ABOUT THE AUTHOR

C. M. Sutter is a crime fiction writer who resides in Florida, although she is originally from California.

She is a member of over fifty writing groups and book clubs. In addition to writing, she enjoys spending time with her family and dog, and you'll often find her writing in airports and on planes as she flies from state to state on family visits.

She is an art enthusiast and loves to create gourd birdhouses, pebble art, and handmade soaps. Gardening, bicycling, fishing, and traveling are a few of her favorite pastimes.

C.M. Sutter

http://cmsutter.com/

Contact C. M. Sutter - http://cmsutter.com/contact/

Pray for Your Life
Detective Mitch Cannon-Savannah Heat Thriller Series, Book 3

A surprise birthday cruise for Mitch Cannon's seventy-year-old mother sets the week in motion.

Mitch had been nominated by his sisters to escort their mom, Mary, on the trip. Feeling railroaded into the task, Mitch is angry, especially since a new case has come up involving a criminal Mitch had a history with, someone who's just shot three people.

Reluctantly, Mitch goes on the trip, and an uncomfortable rift exists between him and his mother. She knows he didn't want to go on the Riviera Maya cruise, but they soon find out that their personal problems are the least of their worries.

Unknown to Mitch, the man he's been after was aware of his every move, and the next six days are something that Mitch, Mary, and most other people would be lucky to even live through.

Has an infamous killer who's never been caught resurfaced after a thirty-year nap? Detective Cannon's worst fear may be coming true—the Savannah Slasher is finally waking up.

See all of C. M. Sutter's books at:
http://cmsutter.com/available-books/

Find C. M. Sutter on Facebook at:
https://www.facebook.com/cmsutterauthor/

Don't want to miss C. M. Sutter's next release?
Sign up for the VIP e-mail list at:
http://cmsutter.com/newsletter/

Pray for Your Life

C. M. Sutter

AUTHOR'S NOTE

This book is a work of fiction by C. M. Sutter. Names, characters, places, and incidents are products of the author's imagination or are used solely for entertainment. Any resemblance to actual events or persons, living or dead, is entirely coincidental.

The scanning, uploading, and distribution of this book via the internet or any other means without the permission of the publisher is illegal and punishable by law. Please purchase only authorized electronic editions, and do not participate in or encourage electronic piracy of copyrighted materials. Your support of the author's rights is appreciated.

Chapter 1

We gathered at the corner diner near our family home that Saturday—Meg, Marie, and me. Meg was the only one who had to drive since Marie and her kids had moved in with me several months ago.

Billie's Lunch Stop was an easy ten-minute walk from my house, and it had always been a favorite family destination when we were growing up.

We'd placed our orders, and Marie and I had offered to pay for Meg's lunch since she had to make the drive. We were on our second cup of coffee before we got down to business.

"Okay, let's each throw out our personal suggestions and then make a decision. We've only got a week before the big day," Marie said. She gave me a nod, meaning I would go first.

"Sure. I think we should have a family party at home and then just us three take Mom out to a real swanky place for supper." I grinned as I stared at my sisters and tried to read their take on my idea. They both swatted the air.

"For a good-looking cop, you're pretty average when it comes to great ideas," Meg said.

Marie nodded. "I'll second that."

I feigned hurt feelings with a frown. "Let's hear your suggestions, then, if your ideas are so superior to mine."

They answered at the same time, obviously in cahoots. "Take Mom on a cruise!"

"What?"

"Yep, she's been talking about taking a cruise forever, and you know damn well she wouldn't go alone."

"Okay, then we'll pay for it if her expensive-as-hell senior-living campus ever plans something like that. They plan group excursions now and then, don't they?"

Marie groaned. "It's not the same, Mitch. Her seventieth birthday—a huge milestone, if you recall—is next Saturday, not someday. It's something she'd want to enjoy with her family, not with a bunch of old women or senior couples."

"Mom *is* a senior, and I doubt that either of you could get away for a weeklong cruise with your whole family when school is still in session. Am I right?"

Meg chuckled. "Don't let Mom hear you call her a senior, but yes, you're absolutely right. That's why you're doing it. You have so much vacation time saved up that you could do a round-the-world cruise, but we aren't asking you to do that."

I felt relieved. "Oh, good."

"A five-day Cozumel, Mexico, cruise would be perfect for you and Mom. That's plenty of time to let her get a taste of cruising. Get her feet wet, so to speak. After that, she can decide if a longer cruise is something she'd want to do in the future or if the five-day trip got the cruising bug out of her system."

My smile quickly faded while my head buzzed with thoughts of how to get out of the cruise my sisters were planning for me.

"I'm sure Mom would be more comfortable with you two instead of me. What do I have in common with a woman her age anyway? We aren't going to belly up to the all-inclusive bar and get drunk, and I'm sure as hell not going to do water aerobics with her." I waited, unamused, as my sisters laughed.

"Come on, bro," Marie said. "Take one for the team. We have commitments, but you don't, and Mom would absolutely love it."

I shook my head. "I'm sure somebody will be murdered by then, plus it's too short of a notice."

Meg turned her palm toward me. "No excuses. There are plenty of other homicide detectives who can take care of your preplanned murders, and it isn't too short of a notice. Consider it an adventure where you and Mom can really get to know each other on a deeper level."

I groaned. "Neither of you are funny."

Marie air-smacked hands with Meg. "Good, then it's settled. You guys drive to Tampa next Thursday, the third of February, board the ship on Friday morning, enjoy the cruise, and are back in Tampa by Tuesday afternoon. Easy peasy. Plus, you owe us six hundred bucks since it's already booked and paid for. We each owe a third."

"What the hell, you guys? I haven't even put in for vacation yet."

Marie looked at Meg, and they burst out laughing. "No worries. I've already cleared those days off for you with

Royce. He knows all about it."

I cursed under my breath and knew I couldn't get out of it. "So it was eighteen hundred in total?"

They both nodded.

"You better hope to God you booked us in separate rooms."

Marie grinned. "Of course we did. You'll love it, and what's five days away? The cruise isn't overly expensive, and it's all-inclusive—eat and drink all you want. Only thing that costs more are land excursions, like visiting Tulum and the other Mayan ruins, but who wouldn't want to check them out, right?"

Meg took her turn. "We'll totally do the family party first, though. That was a great idea, Mitch, so how about tomorrow at your house? You don't have to work, there aren't any new murders on the books, and it'll be perfect weather. Between you, me, Jeff, and Marie, we'll create an outdoor party that Mom will love."

I rubbed my forehead and groaned. "Yeah, whatever."

The waitress brought over our burgers and fries, and while my sisters were ecstatic, I knew that I'd just been totally played.

Chapter 2

The aroma of freshly popped kettle corn filled the kitchen and living room. The three of them—Cynthia and her teenaged kids, Francesca and Calen—got comfortable in their usual spots in front of the TV to watch the last episode of their favorite reality show. It was Sunday night, school was the next day, and at ten o'clock, the kids would have to hit the hay.

Each with their own bowl of popcorn and a soda, they settled in. Calen fast-forwarded through the commercial to the beginning of the show. "Here we go. Everyone shut up."

Francesca huffed. "Nobody is even talking, dummy."

"Okay, okay, shush, both of you," Cynthia said.

The program had just shown the last week's recap when the sound of a car caught Cynthia's attention. It was too close, as if it was in her driveway. She parted the blinds and frowned. She didn't recognize the vehicle until the occupant climbed out. Cynthia leapt to her feet.

"Shit! This can't be happening! No, no, no. Kids, run!"

With a crash, the door burst open and splintered as it bounced off the back wall. A man stepped over the shards of wood and wildly waved a gun at them.

"Mateo! What are you doing here? How did you—" Cynthia tried to shield her kids from the maniac standing several feet away.

"I was released and thought I'd surprise you." He grinned. "Now I'm here to show you who's literally calling the shots."

Cynthia turned toward her kids and screamed, "Run!"

***

Three gunshots rang out, then there was silence. Mateo crossed the room and tapped their bodies with his foot, and when they didn't move, he spat on his ex-girlfriend, walked out, and drove away.

One phone call would ensure his safe passage out of the country, and he had to leave as soon as possible. Mateo called Luis, his right-hand man in the area and his go-to guy for everything he needed or wanted.

"Luis, it's done. Now I need you to book me a flight out of here and make sure it's for tonight. After you've arranged my flight, contact Cruz. Tell him I'm coming and when I'll be landing. Somebody needs to pick me up at the airport. Make sure everyone knows that Mateo Garcia is returning and my position and power will resume as soon as I land on Mexican soil."

Chapter 3

"Yeah, I don't see the humor in it." I glared at Rue as he leaned back in his chair and chuckled.

"Sorry, buddy, but they really got you. I'll admit, that was genius on their part. Have you put in for the vacation time yet?"

I huffed. "I don't have to since Meg and Marie already cleared Thursday, Friday, Monday, and Tuesday with Royce."

Rue laughed even harder. "Good thing I didn't know about it. I might have accidentally let it slip."

"Yeah, great."

Rue tipped his wrist then pushed back his chair. "We better head downstairs. Brass is going to update everyone on that overnight shooting. Word around the water cooler is that the mother and her two teenagers might not make it."

"Shit." I guzzled the rest of my coffee, and we left our office. The meeting area for the entire precinct was downstairs, where there was more room. Our homicide department and SVU would sit in on the meeting together.

We took our seats on the thirty or more folding chairs that faced a podium and large corkboard at the front of the room. What I'd heard about last night's incident was that the shooter was in the wind and the victims hadn't died—yet. If they did, the case would move to us.

Sergeant Timmons from SVU took his place behind the podium and called the room to attention. We were a mix of night and day shift SVU and Homicide detectives as well as fifteen or so officers. Royce and Bleu sat on folding chairs at his side.

Once everyone had quieted down, Timmons cleared his throat with a fist to his mouth. "Okay, listen up, everyone. Either you have heard about or were personally involved with the 911 domestic disturbance call that came in last night. Cynthia Lopez, aged thirty-seven, and her two teenaged kids, Francesca, fifteen, and Calen, thirteen, were gunned down by Ms. Lopez's estranged boyfriend and alleged perp, Mateo Garcia. He was able to evade us by doing what cowards do—run. As of right now, there's an APB out for his arrest, and Ms. Lopez and her kids are in a touch-and-go situation according to the doctors in charge at Mercy Hospital. There's no father on record that we can locate."

Groans sounded throughout the room.

My eyes widened in disbelief. "Did you say Mateo Garcia? As in the Mateo Garcia I arrested numerous times before I came to Homicide?"

"Yes, one and the same, and we need everyone's cooperation in finding that dirtbag." Timmons looked at Bleu and Royce. "We'll keep close tabs on the condition of the mom and kids, but this case could be handed off to Homicide literally at any minute. What we know is that Mateo Garcia is armed, dangerous, and has a lengthy arrest record. The victims were shot with a 9mm handgun, according to the spent casings found at the scene. The hospital confirmed it this morning after removing the slugs, and by the grace of God, all three are still hanging on." Timmons pinned a photo of Mateo to the corkboard. "The neighborhood canvassing began last night, but as we all know, many people won't open their doors after dark. We may have better luck during daylight hours. We need to find a family member or an acquaintance of Mateo's who has the courage to speak up and do the right thing. That man needs to be scooped up quickly before he disappears for good. According to his rap sheet, he has connections in Miami, especially with the 18th Street Gang, also known as Barrio 18 or Calle 18, who operate out of multiple locations such as LA, Central America, Canada, Manila City, and Mexico. As of right now, the Miami PD has been alerted, and state troopers are monitoring the interstates. There's a BOLO out for his 2009 navy-blue Honda Accord, but that doesn't mean he left the area in it." Timmons looked from face to face. "Any questions?"

I spoke up. "Why wasn't he still in prison?"

Timmons continued. "Garcia was serving a five-year stint for drug smuggling. He was released out onto the streets after two years—the same 'overcrowded conditions and prisoner's rights' bs excuse. And as we all know, that's usually when more people are assaulted, hence what happened to Ms.

Lopez and her kids. She wasn't informed of his release, so he took her completely by surprise and ambushed her. Apparently, she had moved on with a decent man in her life and was doing well." Timmons paused as he stared at the podium. "Until last night."

Seconds later, Tracy, from the desk sergeant's counter, walked in, whispered something into Timmons's ear, then left.

Timmons cleared his throat again. "I was about to say this case is completely on SVU for the time being, but now it looks like both departments are involved. Cynthia Lopez just died."

Timmons nodded to Royce, who stepped up to the podium. "Okay, guys and gals, you know what to do. Go track down Cynthia's parents first and tell them what we just learned. They were informed last night, came from Atlanta, and are staying at the Welcome Inn hotel by the airport. Find everyone who knew Cynthia and Mateo as a couple before he went to prison and see if they can shed some light on his whereabouts. You know the drill. Cynthia's phone is in our custody, and we'll go through every contact she has on it and interview them if necessary. We'll check her texts too. Interview her current boyfriend even if he's already been interviewed. Nobody at this point knows that she passed away"—Royce tipped his wrist—"literally twenty minutes ago."

Rue spoke up. "So are we working as a combined team to find Mateo or as independent departments?"

Royce cocked his head and looked from Bleu to

Timmons. "We're all after the same person but for different reasons. SVU for assault with intention to commit murder, and us, for the murder itself. As long as we work hand in hand, I have no problem combining forces."

"Same here," Timmons said. "But we can't step on each other's toes. Everyone has to stay in the loop and work together. Any problem with that?"

Everyone shook their heads, plus it wasn't like we hadn't worked with SVU on many cases in the past, and I was fine with it.

"Cannon and Rue, go talk to the parents and the boyfriend. Lawrence and Bentley, locate the people on the phone's contact list and start talking to them."

Timmons took his turn. "I want all of my day shift guys combing the neighborhood again, and Rich and Denning, I want you to find out who Mateo's cellmate was in prison and interview him."

Royce slapped his hands together and told us to get moving. The meeting was over.

Chapter 4

Rue tipped his head toward me. "So at least tell me yesterday's party was a success."

I grunted. "Yeah, it was great, but since Mom's birthday isn't until next Saturday, we had to explain why we were having the party in advance." I chuckled. "Actually, I haven't seen my mom that excited in years. Maybe the cruise will be fun after all. I mean, what could go wrong in five days?"

Devon lowered his window. Morning condensation had fogged the windshield. "Nothing short of falling overboard."

"Yeah, let's not go there. I'll make sure whenever Mom is on a balcony or near a railing, I'm right next to her."

"Good plan. So Marie is in charge at your house from Thursday until Tuesday night? She's taking care of Gus?"

"Sure, why not? It's actually her house as much as it is mine. I mean, it's going to all of us when Mom passes. Until then, I'm just the steward of the manor."

Rue grinned. "And it's a damn nice manor to be steward of."

When I saw the sign for the Welcome Inn hotel, I clicked my blinker and turned left. My involuntary groan spoke for me. "Guess it's that time. At least Cynthia's parents won't be blindsided by the news in a middle-of-the-night door knock."

"Yeah, that's the only good thing about this visit. We'll catch them before they head to the hospital to ask about Cynthia and the kids' condition. Was Mateo with Cynthia back in the day? Had you ever met her?"

"Thankfully, no. That would have made telling her parents even harder."

I parked the cruiser, and as we walked, I noticed the overflowing outdoor ashtray just steps from the hotel entrance. I wrinkled my nose and yanked open the door, and we entered the lobby.

A redheaded reservations clerk wearing a name tag with Karen embossed on it called out to us right away. "Can I help you?"

I approached the counter and flipped open my ID wallet, exposing my badge. "We're looking for Mr. and Mrs. Joseph Lopez. I believe they checked in overnight."

A voice came from behind my right shoulder. "I'm Dina Lopez."

I turned. "Mrs. Lopez, Cynthia's mother?"

"Yes, that's me."

"Ma'am, I'm Detective Cannon, and this is my partner, Detective Rue. May we speak to you and your husband?"

"He's still asleep, but yes, please follow me."

The look on her face told me she knew why we were there. Tears pooled in her eyes and slid down her cheeks.

"It's bad news, isn't it?"

"How about we talk to you and your husband together,

ma'am?" Rue said as we entered the elevator.

"Please, just call me Dina."

The elevator doors parted at the second floor, and after stepping out, Dina turned right. "We're in room 214."

When we reached the door, she asked if we could give her a few minutes—she needed to wake her husband.

"Sure thing, ma'am. Just let us in when you're ready."

With a stiff upper lip, she entered the room and closed the door at her back. My phone vibrated in my pocket as we waited. Royce had sent a text with Cynthia's boyfriend's name, address, and phone number. He said he'd done a background check on him already, and Daniel Ruiz was clean. I fired off a quick thanks, sent it, and dropped the phone into my pocket.

Seconds later, the door squeaked open, and a teary-eyed Dina asked us in. The room was the typical hotel double with two queen-sized beds. One had been slept in, and the other was untouched. Dina and her husband, Joe, sat on the unmade bed and offered us the other. We faced them, and Rue began.

"Mr. Lopez, are you familiar with guns?"

"Yes, I am. I'm a retired corrections officer and worked at USP Atlanta for seventeen years."

"Then you know the kind of damage a 9mm can do to a human body."

"I do. Are you telling us that Cynthia and the kids are dead?"

"Sir—"

Dina's voice caught in her throat. "Just tell us. We're already expecting the worst."

"Yes, ma'am." Rue took in a deep breath. "According to last night's first responder's account, Cynthia was found lying in front of Francesca and Calen. It's likely she took the majority of the injuries, although they were all critically wounded. I'm sorry to have to tell you this, but Cynthia didn't make it."

Dina covered her face with her hands and broke down. "She was our baby, the youngest child, and the most innocent. We had no idea that monster was released from prison. How can they do that without warning Cynthia? She and the kids could have stayed with us in Atlanta. But now it's too late. She's dead!"

I stared at my shoes. "I'm so sorry, ma'am. We're going to do everything in our power to capture him and send him right back to prison, hopefully to death row, where he'll never see the light of day again. Our question is, do you know anything about Mateo that might help us find him?"

Joe spoke up. "We met him once three years ago. We were visiting Cynthia, and he showed up unannounced, angry, and yelling at her. He didn't like it when she wasn't at his beck and call. He only stuck around for ten minutes and then stormed off. We found out a month later that he beat her up after that. We pleaded with Cindy to get rid of him, and she tried, but he kept showing up until he was finally sent to prison on unrelated charges." Joe cocked his head at us. "Why is it that men are never held criminally responsible for abusing women?"

"I hate to say this, Joe, but it's mostly because the women are afraid to press charges for fear of retaliation. It's a vicious cycle of abuse that only stops if the perp is incarcerated or the victim moves away."

Dina huffed. "But he was incarcerated until the system let him go. He still got to my daughter and murdered her!"

There was nothing I could say to ease their pain. Everything Dina and Joe had said was true. The system failed Cynthia terribly, and she paid the ultimate price with her life. The kids might, too, and the only thing we could do to get justice for them was to find Mateo Garcia.

"What about the kids?" Joe asked. "They have no mother now, and they're both critically wounded."

"It's too early to know. Both Francesca and Calen are in ICU, meaning no visitors, but you can look at them through the glass wall," I said. "We'll make sure to clear you with the lead in that department. Because the kids were shot, we can't allow anyone other than family to see or inquire about them."

Dina blew her nose then wiped her eyes. "Where is Cynthia?"

"She's in the hospital's morgue. There's no need for an autopsy unless you request one since we already know what killed her."

Joe shook his head. "We just want to bury our daughter and let her rest in peace."

"And we'll let you know when that's possible. We will need you to identify her, though, sometime today. We'll escort you to the hospital's morgue, where you'll make the ID and sign a few papers. After that, we'll go to ICU, inquire about the kids, and make sure you're on the approved visitors' list."

Dina nodded. "Thank you, Detectives. They're at Mercy Hospital?"

"That's correct, ma'am," Rue said.

"Okay. Please give us a few hours of private time to grieve our loss."

I handed my card to Dina and said for them to text me when they were heading our way, and we left. In the car, I programmed the boyfriend's address into my phone but called first. I had no idea if he was at home, at work, or somewhere else, but I was sure he didn't know that Cynthia had died.

Danny Ruiz answered on the second ring. "Hello?"

"Is this Daniel Ruiz?" I asked.

"Yes. Who's asking?"

"This is Detective Cannon calling from the Savannah PD. We'd like to speak with you about Cynthia and if she's ever discussed her previous relationship."

"You mean with that nutcase, Mateo Garcia?"

"He's the one. We'll need a half hour of your time since you haven't been interviewed yet. Where can we meet you?"

"You can come to my home. I didn't have the will or energy to go to work today. I'm going to head to the hospital soon, though."

"There's no visitation allowed in ICU, Mr. Ruiz, especially for shooting victims, unless law enforcement is present, the visitors are family, and the doctor allows it."

"Um, then—"

"How about we come to your house now and talk?"

"Okay, I guess. My address is—"

"We've got your address. We'll be there in fifteen minutes."

At ten o'clock, we reached Daniel's impressive two-story on East Forty-Fifth Street. I was surprised that he lived in such a nice neighborhood, made up mostly of large older homes on tree-lined streets. They were the kind of properties I pictured belonging to retired doctors and attorneys. I would make sure to ask him his occupation when we sat down.

I pulled along the curb and killed the engine, checked the address again, then dipped my head and looked through the passenger-side window. "Supposedly, that redbrick is his."

Rue raised his brows. "You sure? Seems to be a night-and-day difference from dating a drug smuggler and gang member to this."

My shrug conveyed my uncertainty. "It's the address Royce gave me. In hindsight, I should have let Ruiz rattle it off anyway."

Devon opened the passenger door and climbed out. "No time like the present to find out."

Perfectly manicured shrubbery lined the slate sidewalk that ended at a massive wooden door. I clanked the doorknocker twice, and we waited. Within seconds, the door swung open, and a nicely dressed fortysomething man welcomed us in.

"I take it you're the detectives?"

I confirmed it with my badge. "We are, and you're Daniel Ruiz?"

He nodded. "Please come inside. We can talk in the study."

The fifty-foot walk from the foyer to the study raised my curiosity even more. The house—at least the part I saw—was tastefully furnished. I couldn't imagine why Cynthia had ever dated a thug when she could have been with someone like Daniel all along.

After we were seated, Daniel began. "So, what can I tell you about my relationship with Cynthia or what I know of Mateo Garcia?"

The interview would come soon enough, but first, Daniel needed to know the main reason for our visit.

"Before we ask any questions, we're here for another reason," I said.

His face went pale. "Did something more happen?"

"We're sorry to tell you that Cynthia passed away this morning."

He buried his face in his hands. "I didn't even get the chance to see her, to say I love her, to say I'm sorry."

"Sorry?" Rue asked. "For what?"

"For not being there to protect her and the kids last night. I planned to spend the evening with them, but I had to close the restaurant. If only—"

"Nobody could have known what was going to happen. The prison system failed her. They didn't tell her that Mateo was released."

"Are the kids going to make it? Do they even know their mother is dead?"

"Not to our knowledge, and so far, they're hanging on. We're going to the hospital later to walk Cynthia's parents through the ID process. We'll check on the kids then." I sucked in a deep breath. "But right now, we have questions for you."

He sniffed then stared at his shoes. "Yeah, go ahead. I'm an open book."

I took the lead that time, and Rue wrote down the notes.

"First, how long had you and Cynthia been dating?"

"About a year, I guess." He gave us a weak smile. "I remember when I first laid eyes on her. She came into my restaurant because of the Help Wanted sign in the window. We were looking for servers, but I hired her as a hostess instead. I've seen how hard our waitresses work—long hours, dealing with disgruntled customers, and so on."

"You own a restaurant?"

He nodded. "I took over the reins four years ago. It's been in my family for thirty years."

"What's the name?"

"Cantina Ruiz."

I raised my brows. "That's your place?"

Danny nodded again. "So you know of it?"

"I've eaten there plenty of times. Great food, man."

"Thank you."

That explained Danny's home. His restaurant was always packed, and their food was top-notch.

He continued. "It didn't take long before I asked Cynthia out, and we've been a couple ever since. I love those kids like they're my own."

"I'm sure you do. Did you ever meet Mateo, or had she talked of him?"

"Yes and no." He looked up. "She told me about him after we began dating, but I never met the guy. I don't think she felt safe going out with anyone else until she knew without a doubt that he'd spend the next five years in prison. Cynthia's entire outlook on life had changed after that. She moved to a different house, she was happy, and she stopped looking over her shoulder."

"Did she ever say how she got involved with the likes of him?"

"From what she told me, she met him through a coworker at her previous job. She said Mateo came across as a nice guy at first, but you know how abusers are. Nice for a while and then look out."

"Do you know the names of any of his friends?"

"No. I keep my distance from that type, although we do get some rough characters in the restaurant now and then. The only name I've heard is Luis, and he's the guy who introduced Cynthia to Mateo when she worked as a receptionist at Tony's Tires on East Anderson Street. I don't know if he was related to Mateo or just a friend."

"Okay, that helps."

We offered our condolences, mentioned again that Cynthia's parents were in town in case he wanted to contact them, and said we'd let him know the condition of the kids as soon as we spoke to their doctor.

Concern covered Danny's face as I passed my card to him. "Will you get Mateo, Detectives?"

"I sure as hell hope so, buddy. That man should have never been released from prison in the first place, and now—" I shook my head, patted him on the shoulder, and we left.

Chapter 5

As I pulled away from the curb, I checked the time. It was pushing eleven o'clock.

"Let's head in, update Royce, and see what the rest of the team has come up with. After that, we'll dig further into that Luis guy."

As I drove, I wondered whether Cynthia's murder could get me out of the cruise, but after seeing how excited my mom was yesterday, there was no way I could bail on her. My sisters would never forgive me. Besides, I doubted that we would be refunded the costs of the cruise and land excursion on such short notice.

There were only two more workdays before Mom and I headed to Tampa. Mateo might or might not be caught by then, but with SVU and our homicide department working on his capture, being short one detective wouldn't likely hinder the investigation.

I rolled into the parking lot and killed the engine, then once we reached the second floor, Rue and I headed straight for Royce's office. We nearly hit him head-on as he was walking out.

"Where's the fire?"

Royce cursed as he rushed past us then waved for us to follow. We fell in line behind him—the hallway wasn't wide enough for the three of us.

"Somebody messed up. They were supposed to red-flag Mateo's passport, but it showed up in Miami for a flight to Chetumal, Mexico. He's gone, and he has a lot of status in Mexico. From there, he could go anywhere without us ever finding him since Chetumal is right on the border of Belize. His gang acquaintances will make sure they keep him safe and off the grid. Mateo has connections all over Mexico and Central America."

I frowned. "How did he get a passport to begin with? Felons who deal in international drug smuggling can't get them."

"He must have had one before he went to prison. Maybe somebody renewed it for him, or maybe it's fake. Who knows?" Royce threw up his arms as he stormed down the stairs.

"Where are we going?"

"To the first box. SVU picked up Mateo's best friend, Luis Ortega, on some old warrant. They're talking to him now."

"I wonder if he's the same Luis that Daniel told us about. He worked at Tony's Tires on East Anderson."

Royce huffed. "And still does."

We took seats in the observation room, where Royce flipped on the audio switch. We got comfortable and listened in on the interview. While looking at Luis, I noticed dozens of tattoos on his arms, notably the 18th Street Gang symbol front and center on his right forearm.

"He's not going to talk," I said.

Royce gave me a side-eyed glance. "You're suddenly psychic?"

"Nope, just recognize a gang tattoo when I see one, or a dozen. If he talks and is found out to be a snitch, he's as good as dead."

"Shit." Royce clenched his fists.

"Mexico will extradite Mateo to the US, won't they?" Rue asked.

"Sure, if they ever find him, but he'll likely move from country to country with fake IDs compliments of his gang affiliations." Royce grumbled. "All he needed to do was successfully get out of the US, and he did that with flying colors. Local cops can't chase him around the globe. Only the FBI can do that, and I'm sure they have bigger fish to fry."

I stared through the glass at the man who'd likely helped Mateo get out of the country. We were losing our focus on the victims, though—Cynthia, who was now deceased, and her critically injured teenaged kids. I wondered what would happen to them if they survived, and I intended to discuss that with the grandparents later.

After listening to the interview, Royce shooed us off, saying everything at the precinct was under control. SVU had a half-dozen officers canvassing Cynthia's neighborhood, and others were going through her phone's contact list. Lawrence and Bentley had already spoken with the woman who made the 911 call after hearing the gunshots.

"Okay, we're heading to the hospital, then. The Lopezes need to ID Cynthia's body, and I'm sure they want an update on the kids. If allowed, we'll take them into the ICU wing to peek at them through the glass."

With a nod, Royce said to keep him posted. He would try to make contact with the US Embassy in Mexico City to see if there was a way to arrest Mateo Garcia and get him into custody there, if the local authorities could even track him down.

With that, Rue and I headed to the hospital to meet with Dina and Joe Lopez. I'd gotten a text saying they would be waiting for us at twelve thirty under the portico outside the building's entrance. We had just enough time to grab a burger and fries at a nearby drive-through, chow them down, and get on our way.

As I drove, Rue called the hospital for an update. We didn't want to walk in on any surprises. As of ten minutes ago, both kids were considered in extremely critical condition but hanging on. After reaching the hospital's parking lot, I lowered the visor and looked in the mirror. I didn't want any telltale food on my face when we met with Cynthia's parents.

Once I was satisfied that no food lingered on my mouth, we left the cruiser and crossed the lot. I pointed as I saw Dina and Joe sitting under the portico on a bench, just like they'd said they would be.

"There they are. This is going to be a hell of a bad day for them."

Rue agreed, and once we reached them, we escorted them

inside. The lower level of the hospital was where the morgue, autopsy room, and resident coroner's office were located. I knew the room would be cold, stark, and unwelcoming, yet who would want to be welcomed there anyway? I was glad to see Dina had a sweater draped over her arm. I pressed the *L* on the elevator, the doors opened, and we boarded. After the doors closed and a slight jostle, we descended.

"It's chilly in there." I pointed my chin at her sweater. "You might want to put that on."

"Thank you."

Downstairs, we met with Don Pressley, the hospital's coroner. A few courtesies and introductions were exchanged, then he said he would prepare Cynthia for viewing and identification. It wouldn't be an easy few minutes for the Lopezes. Their daughter would roll out of a stainless steel refrigerated drawer the size of a narrow coffin for them to ID her, then she'd be rolled back in. No sitting with her, holding her hand, or kissing her cold skin. A nod was all Don needed. After papers were signed and the family received a handful of death certificates and her personal effects, they would leave. We'd be in and out in under thirty minutes. I knew the process, and I knew it was a matter-of-fact, to-the-point procedure, yet Don was a kind and caring man. After he offered his condolences, we would be on our way to the third floor ICU wing.

Once Don escorted Dina and Joe back, Rue and I waited on the guest chairs in his office. Although the process was far from personal—and short at that—it would allow a private moment between the parents and their daughter.

Minutes later, they were back, both with watery red eyes. They sat, signed the necessary documents, and were given the death certificates. I gave Don a thank-you nod, and we left.

From the looks of it, Dina and Joe needed a few minutes to regroup. I suggested coffee in the cafeteria before we continued to ICU.

After taking our seats and ordering four coffees, I asked about the kids and the plans for them if they came out of their predicament whole and capable of living normal lives. I hadn't asked Joe or Dina's ages, but they looked to be in their late fifties. I had no idea whether they were prepared to, or wanted to, take two possibly handicapped kids into their home and their lives on a full-time basis. If not, the children would probably go into the foster care system, where oftentimes, life was as bad as living on the streets.

Their response was what I'd expected, but at least I'd planted the seed and given them something to think about. Because the situation was volatile and nobody knew how the kids would turn out if they lived, Joe and Dina said they didn't know what to do. They were trying to get through the day, then the week, and after that was still an unknown.

We finished our coffees, they cleared their heads, and we went upstairs. At the nurses' station, we got them signed up as approved visitors to the wing. They could see the kids through the glass, but that was as far as they could go. Francesca and Calen were hooked up to every kind of IV and monitor, and according to the doctor on duty, they would need additional surgeries in a few days if they made it through the night. The next twenty-four hours were critical.

We parted ways at two o'clock, with us heading to the precinct and Joe and Dina to the hotel. They'd asked about Cynthia's house and belongings, but because the home was still considered a crime scene, they weren't allowed inside yet. They said they would be in Savannah all week if we needed to speak to them again. With that, we said our goodbyes and left.

Chapter 6

I had a day and a half of work to go before leaving thoughts of Mateo Garcia in the rearview mirror. My mom and I would be hopping into my Corvette and heading to Tampa. The drive was a good five plus hours depending on traffic conditions, road construction, accidents, and the number of stops we made. I wondered where our conversations would take us or if she'd doze off after ten minutes in the car. Time would tell, but I was curious to hear about the conversation Royce had with the US Embassy in Mexico.

Back at the station, Royce recounted what the embassy liaison, Manny Tropp, had told him over the phone after receiving the email with Mateo's criminal record and the police report from last night. He would pass all that information on to the local police and let them know that Mateo Garcia had flown to Chetumal overnight and was somewhere in their country. Because he hadn't been part of any criminal activity in the last ten hours or so, they would have no idea where he might have gone or if he'd already left Mexico and moved into Belize or Guatemala. He literally could be anywhere and completely off the grid with the help of his drug-running amigos. Manny had assured Royce that the embassy would distribute Mateo's rap sheet and photo to the local police in Playa del Carmen, which had the consular agency nearest Chetumal, but unless Mateo committed a crime in a city where the police force was strong, he would likely slip through the cracks and never be apprehended.

Royce was fit to be tied. Not only had the prison system released a known gang affiliate—an international drug smuggler—but his passport hadn't been flagged. That gave Mateo a free pass out of the country after he shot three people, with one already classified as a murder.

We were at a standstill, and Cynthia's death would likely be a murder without justice, at least in the here and now. Twenty years down the road, Mateo might show up. Usually, when criminals thought the world had forgotten them, that was when they were caught doing something stupid like stealing a pack of cigarettes or driving ten miles over the speed limit. All we could do was process the scene like any other, collect evidence, interview people, and hope the kids lived.

"How about putting his face on those most wanted criminal TV shows?" I asked.

Royce sighed. "We will, but it takes time to get a spot on one of those programs. Meanwhile, we'll air his face on the local news and on social media and hope news of the shootings spreads throughout the country. That man will run out of hiding places in time."

"But time isn't what we have a lot of if we hope to get a conviction," Devon said. "Without sightings of him, the news will fade, and the leads we get will become as cold as ice."

"And that could happen, but I truly believe criminals get their just reward sooner or later. He'll be caught and serve his time. It's just a matter of when."

I cocked my head as I thought, and Rue apparently noticed.

"Something percolating in there?"

"Yeah. Now that Cynthia is dead, we can interview that Luis character too. We have a dog in this fight just as much as SVU does."

"True, but like you said earlier, they're gang brothers, and he isn't going to give up Mateo."

"SVU didn't mention that Cynthia was dead. The murder part doesn't fall under their department."

Royce agreed. "Right. So?"

"So, I'll push him harder. I'll let him know that his name came up as the person who facilitated Mateo's safe passage out of the country. He'll be on the hook as an accomplice to murder."

"Do you think those gangbangers haven't murdered before? A good portion of prisoners in federal lockup are gang members who've killed plenty of people."

"But there's one difference."

Rue raised his brows. "What's that?"

"Luis isn't in prison yet, and according to his rap sheet, he's never been beyond the county jail system. I can put the fear of God in him and make sure he thinks he'll be heading to USP Florence, the worst prison in the country. I'll let him know that prisoners are shivved there daily, especially ones who kill women and kids. I doubt if I'll get a full minute-by-minute account of Mateo's whereabouts, but I may get something. We should definitely bug his phone too. There's a chance that Mateo might call him from wherever he's hiding out. He's a career criminal for God's sake and one who needs to have a permanent residence in a prison cell, no matter whether the system is overcrowded or not."

Royce shook his head as he fidgeted with a paperclip. "Criminals are smarter than that. Mateo isn't going to call anyone in the US. He'll go through five people in different locations before his message ever gets to Luis, if he has a message for him at all."

"Yeah, maybe, but I can still try to get something out of him."

"Okay, go ahead, but make sure you threaten him with enough to set him back on his heels."

I grinned and turned to Rue. "Want to pitch in?"

"Hell yeah. Sitting around stewing isn't getting us anywhere."

Chapter 7

I asked Jack to return Luis to the first box. I wanted to have a go at him. The guy was cagey and not easily fooled, but I was tougher, smarter, and knew my way around the law far better than he did. I could scare the bejesus out of most criminals with my tried-and-true tactics.

Tomorrow was my last day of work before I was out of the game until the following week. Anything could happen during that time, including two more murder charges if the kids didn't make it.

I knew Mateo, which gave me an advantage I could use to mess with Luis's mind. Rue and I took fifteen minutes to plan our attack and the words most likely to frighten Mateo's sidekick into giving us something. We could lie—it didn't matter—and anything and everything was on the table. Cops got a pass on that in order to gain much-needed information from dirtbags like Luis.

If only Cynthia was here. She probably heard a lot of Luis's stories during the years she worked with him at the tire shop.

It was time to go hard at Luis and not let up. It was time to throw everything at Mateo, including my past experiences with him. I'd make sure Luis knew that his *ese*, his man, wasn't faithful to anyone, including him. Mateo would throw anyone under the bus to save his own skin, and it was just a matter of time before Luis found himself in prison anyway, compliments of Mateo Garcia.

We entered the box where Luis was cuffed to the table bar. He wore an orange jumpsuit even though we would have to cut him loose in forty-eight hours unless SVU came up with something that would stick. That old disturbing-the-peace warrant wouldn't hold him there for long.

I started since I would be the worst of us two. We wouldn't play the good cop, bad cop game. Everyone knew that was bs, but we could be the bad and badder cops in the room.

Rue and I plopped down across from Luis at the stainless steel table bolted to the floor. I held the police jacket listing his previous arrests. I smacked the folder on the table, loud and hard.

"What's up, Luis?"

He shrugged. "What do you want? I've already sat across from two other cops, told them nothing, and now I'm missing my siesta."

I looked at Rue and chuckled. "This asshole thinks he's running the show. Similar to how Mateo thinks too. Are you his bitch, his student, his little boy?" I cocked my head, held eye contact with him, and grinned. "Or are you his little girl?"

"Up yours, Pig."

I continued. "You see, Luis, what you don't know is that Mateo and I go way back, probably back to when you were still pissing your pants." I cracked my knuckles. "Or maybe you still do. Guess you haven't heard the news."

"Yeah, what's that?"

"Cynthia Lopez died this morning. You two used to be friends when she worked at Tony's, right?"

He shrugged again.

"The thing that perplexes me is that after Mateo went to prison, Cynthia moved to another part of town. He wouldn't have known where she lived. She broke contact with everyone he knew, but—"

"But what?"

"But for some reason, you kept tabs on her. Common sense tells me it's because Mateo ordered you to."

Luis huffed. "I don't take orders from anyone."

Rue and I laughed. "That's rich. You're the one who told Mateo where she moved and that she was dating someone else. It's the only way he could have known."

"Okay, so what?"

"So that makes you an accomplice to murder, idiot."

Instinctively, he tried to raise his hands in protest, but the cuffs jerked them back.

With a chuckle, I leaned in closer. "Good one, idiot. Here's your problem, buddy. You're going to take the rap for Cynthia's murder since Mateo fled the country. Like I said, I know the guy, and he isn't loyal to anyone. He'd slit your throat like a stuck pig if it made his life easier. From what I've heard, life along the Riviera Maya is pretty sweet."

Rue took his turn. "And with a little digging, I bet we could track the payment of that airplane ticket right back to you or someone you put Mateo in touch with." Rue gave me a raised brow before continuing. "You ever been to Colorado, Luis?"

"No."

"Man, it's a beautiful state and definitely eye candy."

"Then maybe I'll go on vacation there as soon as you pigs release me."

"How about a trip there really soon, all expenses paid?"

"Sounds good to me."

"Great!" Rue scratched his cheek. "Weren't you saying something earlier about USP Florence, Mitch?"

"Ah, that's right. The worst prison in the United States, and it just happens to be in Colorado. You're in luck, Luis, because I have sway with the prison board. I can recommend sending you there and"—I patted my own shoulder—"I usually get my way. Unfortunately, newcomers aren't well-received there. They tend to get shivved sometime during the first week, and that's especially true for people like you."

Luis chuckled. "I don't scare easily."

"No? By the way your face went pale, I'd say we're doing our job. Like I said before, the Caribbean coast of Mexico is a great place to settle down, but Florence, Colorado? If you're lucky, you may get a glimpse of the mountains through your sliver of a window, but you probably won't live long enough to see them." I opened his police file. "It's a real shame, Luis. Until now, all your crimes have been small potatoes. You've been spared the supermax but not anymore. I'll make the call to the prison board right now and give them a heads-up. You're going down for one and possibly three murders while Mateo lounges with an umbrella drink in hand on some beach in Mexico. He's protected by his real eses." I stood to leave.

"He's not—"

I turned back. "Not what?" I sat down. "This is your one and only chance to talk. Tell us now or saddle up. You'll be spending life, no matter how short it is, with the real cowboys in Florence."

Luis groaned.

I rattled my fingers against the table to unnerve him. "The clock is ticking. It's you or him. Decide now."

"Okay, okay. I'm not taking a murder rap for Mateo. I bought two burner phones and got them set up for Mateo and me weeks before he left the country. That way, we could communicate after the deed was done."

"The deed? You mean the shootings?"

Luis nodded.

"And?"

"And he's going to move around."

I yelled while I slapped the table. "To where!"

"I don't know."

After shoving my chair back, I stood again. "Let's go. This chickenshit isn't talking." I growled in Luis's face. "But you are taking a trip to Colorado before the week's end."

"Wait! He said something about moving north or farther inland. That's all I know, I swear. He said nobody would look for him there."

"Where's your burner phone?"

"Release me today. Otherwise, you'll never find it."

I laughed. "Like I said before, you aren't calling the shots."

"Then I want a lawyer."

Chapter 8

I stormed out of the box with Rue taking up the rear.

"We got something. Now all we need to do is find that phone."

"Luis could be making up all of it, Mitch. Mateo may have gone to Belize and Luis is trying to throw us off his track."

"Maybe so, but that phone will tell us everything we need to know, and I only have one more day to work." I waved him toward me. "Come on."

"Where to?"

"The lockers. I want to go through his personal effects."

Jack opened the locker that contained Luis's phone, wallet, clothes, and shoes. I removed his phone and wallet and had Jack catalog everything in the wallet, then we headed to our tech department. Inside, Tom was hard at work.

"How long will it take for you to get into this phone?" I handed it to him.

"Password protected?"

"Yep, and he just lawyered up."

"If he isn't talking, I'd say it's faster to find the last bill, get the phone number and the service provider's name, and request a printout to be emailed to you."

"Yeah, that's fine but not doable in twenty-four hours, and they'd want a warrant. Most people don't get paper bills anyway. He said he bought two burner phones, but I don't know if that's true or not."

"Royce can get someone to search his house for it."

"Also need a warrant."

Tom stared at the wallet in my hand. "Did you check for a credit card in there?"

"Not yet. Jack cataloged everything in it before he gave it to me." I flipped open the wallet and found a card. I pulled it out, tapped it against my hand, and tried to think of a way to access his purchases. There wasn't a way without a warrant, but going that route could be the fastest way to secure those burner phone records and learn where the calls were going to and coming from. "Thanks, buddy. I better get Royce on those warrants as fast as I can."

Rue and I raced upstairs and went through all the options with our sergeant. The fastest way to get to the burner phone records was to see if the phones actually existed, and that would be through credit card records. Royce called Judge Laughlin and said we needed warrants as fast as humanly possible. Finding our runaway murderer depended on it.

As a precaution, Royce asked for warrants for the credit card records, the phones, and Luis's house. If one search was a dead end, hopefully, another would be a success. It was midafternoon by the time the warrants came in. Royce rushed into our office, said he had them, then asked for the credit card's 800 number. He said he could get the right person on the phone faster than we as detectives could. I read the number off the back of the card as he called from my desk phone.

When he got through, he set the phone to Speaker. It took only two transfers to get to the person in charge. After Royce read the warrant information to the supervisor, he was put on hold while the supervisor looked up Luis's purchases. He came back to the phone in under five minutes.

"Sergeant Royce?"

"Yep, still here."

"Okay, it looks like Mr. Ortega purchased two phones at a Save Mart in Savannah on December seventeenth."

"Does it say which store?"

"Yes, on South Abercorn."

"Great, and now I'll need his purchases for the entire year emailed to me."

"Not a problem, sir."

Sarge rattled off his email, thanked the supervisor, and hung up. "There. Now you two need to go to that store, have them pull up the receipt, the serial number details, and phone numbers issued to them, and find out who the service provider is. Meanwhile, I'll have Lawrence and Bentley go to Luis's house and start digging through everything to see if they can find that phone." He tipped his head toward the hallway. "Let's go. You need that warrant for the phone information, and it's sitting on my desk."

We walked with Royce and scooped up the warrant to present to the manager in the phone department and find out everything we needed to know. If Lawrence and Bentley were lucky enough to find Luis's burner phone, we would play the same game with Mateo that criminals played time and time again—pretend to be the phone owner and correspond only through text messages. We would act like Luis, and Mateo wouldn't be the wiser. Once we got the actual phone numbers, I planned to call Bentley, give him Luis's number, and have him call it. If it was set to ring and was anywhere inside the house, they would hear it.

We headed to Save Mart with the warrant in hand. After ten minutes of explaining what we wanted to a salesclerk who stared at us as if we were Martians, we finally got the department manager to come out and address the warrant and what we needed from them.

We gave the manager the name of the person who purchased the phones, Luis Ortega, the date the purchase was made, and the credit card used. With that information and a few taps of the computer keys, he was able to pull up the phone numbers, service provider used, and the serial numbers. After he printed out the information for us, we thanked him for his help and left.

Back in the cruiser and sitting in the parking lot, I called Bentley's cell phone. "Hey, pal, are you at Luis's house, and have you found that phone?"

"We are, but we haven't found it, although we just got here ten minutes ago."

"Okay. I have both of the burner phone numbers for you, but I don't know which one Luis used and which is Mateo's. We could call the service provider, issue a warrant for their records, and see where the calls originated from on which phone, but that'll take more time."

"Not a problem. I'll block my number before I try either of them and then see if someone answers. It they do, it's likely the phone Mateo has."

"Yeah, that'll work. Keep us posted."

We returned to the precinct, where Royce told us a public defender was downstairs talking to Luis. Unless they came up with a deal that included telling us where the burner phone was, Luis would remain in jail, I'd be on vacation, and the search for Mateo would stall, giving him even more time to slip deeper into the unknown areas of Mexico or Central America.

We took seats on Royce's guest chairs and told him what we'd learned.

"We got the phone numbers, which I forwarded to Bentley," I said.

"Good, then it's only a matter of time before they find that burner phone."

Rue shook his head. "Not if it isn't on Luis's property."

I had to disagree. "Luis needs to stay in touch with Mateo, so that means the phone has to be within hearing distance at all times. So, not in his car, buried in the backyard, or hidden in his garage. It's somewhere in the house, where he'd have easy access to it at all times."

Royce scratched his cheek. "Yep, that's the only thing that makes sense. Why don't you two go lend a hand at Luis's house? If that burner phone is set to vibrate instead of ring, it's going to take more time to track it down."

I jerked my head toward the door. "What about Luis and his attorney?"

"Luis can sit on ice for a while. We aren't going to give him a deal for the phone's location if we're able to find it ourselves."

I looked back and tapped the doorframe before walking out. "Good point."

Chapter 9

I called Bentley again before we set out. There wasn't a good reason to head their way if they'd already located the phone. He said they hadn't.

The day was going too quickly for my liking. I would feel more comfortable leaving for a vacation if we had the investigation and Mateo Garcia's location wrapped up neatly by tomorrow, but things didn't always go my way. The proverbial wrench was thrown into the mix more often than I cared to admit.

Fifteen minutes later, Rue and I arrived at the house Luis lived in. The neighborhood had seen better days, and every home on the block could be considered a tear down.

I stared out the windshield. "Wow."

Rue turned my way. "I was just thinking the same thing. Makes you wonder what he does with his paycheck."

I snickered. "I know one thing for sure."

"Yeah, what's that?"

"He doesn't invest it into that house."

The home was a small white one-story structure devoid of nearly all paint and was mostly weatherworn gray clapboards.

The front window on the left was boarded up, likely with broken glass behind it or none at all. The yard was a mix of dead grass and tall weeds. Two tires lay next to the porch for no reason I could think of unless the garage was so full of junk that there wasn't an extra inch of space.

The cruiser that Bentley and Lawrence had arrived in was parked along the curb, and Luis's beater of a vehicle sat in the one-car driveway. I parked between Luis's house and the dilapidated one next door, and we headed up the sidewalk. I banged on Luis's closed front door then walked in.

"It's us, Cannon and Rue," I called out.

Lawrence and Bentley came down the hallway and joined us in the living room.

I plopped down on the threadbare couch cushion and grimaced when I hit a spring. "Seriously, what the hell? The guy is collecting juice off of drug trades, plus he has an actual job. Why would anyone choose to live this way?"

Bentley groaned. "The rest of the house is just as bad. I thought the bed sheets were brown, but it's actually just grime."

I wrinkled my face at the thought. "Well, the sooner we find that phone, the sooner we can get the hell out of here. Where have you looked?"

Lawrence fielded that question. "We eliminated the back porch, the garage, and both the bedrooms. Everything else is fair game."

"Have you figured out which phone number belongs to Luis?" Rue asked.

"Yep, we're pretty certain it's the one that ends in 5402.

I called the other first, a man picked up, and I hung up. It had to be Mateo."

"Good. At least he answers his burner," I said. "And once we find the one Luis uses, we'll have it made."

Rue rubbed his chin as he looked across the living room. "So we have the bathroom, the hallway, the living room, and the kitchen left?"

"And the coat closet and laundry room."

"Shouldn't take too long."

"Except we would have heard the phone ring if it was in ring mode."

I let out a loud sigh. "Meaning it's on vibrate."

"Exactly."

"Then we better perk up our ears. It has to vibrate loud enough that he heard it."

"Unless he changed the setting immediately and stashed the phone if he actually saw SVU coming toward the house."

I nodded. That scenario was a good possibility. "So, if that's the case, he has a quick and well-hidden place he can stash it in less than a minute. Let's begin in here, where he likely was when SVU came calling. Use your imagination and think hard since the hiding place could be in plain sight."

We scanned the room thoroughly. Against the living room's back wall was a couch. Next to it was a god-awful upholstered side chair, with a TV tray as an end table alongside it, and in front of the grouping sat a coffee table. Against the opposite wall was an entertainment center with a TV that was at least ten years old in the largest opening. That was flanked by shelves of hand-me-down knickknacks, a few photographs, and an assortment of hardcover books with Spanish titles. A thick black Bible sat beneath the books.

The couch cushions were tossed, unzipped, and gone through. The rugs were moved in case they had loose floorboards with secret compartments beneath them. That phone had to be located somewhere that Luis could get to it fast. Rue looked through the coat closet and checked every pocket of the jackets hanging inside. He went through the few boxes on the shelf—nothing.

"Okay, there's four of us. Pick a side of the room, everyone be as quiet as possible, and Bentley, you call the phone again. If anyone hears the slightest buzz, raise your hand."

We each took a side, and mine opened to the kitchen. Bentley had already programmed the two numbers to his cell phone. He tapped the number listed as Luis. We held our breath and perked our ears, but the dogs barking outside didn't help matters. I looked from face to face, and everyone shrugged.

"Let's work together since these doors and windows must be made of paper. All four of us take one wall at a time. Stand a few feet apart, make the call, and listen again."

We began along the front of the living room, where the boarded-up window was. Bentley called the number— nothing buzzed. After pushing away the couch, we stood against the back wall, checked behind the velvet wall art showing dogs playing poker, then waited for Bentley to call again. No vibrating sound. The next wall wasn't much of one, a half wall at best because it opened to the kitchen, but still, we heard nothing. The last wall held the entertainment center. Before removing everything and pulling the cabinet away from the wall, Bentley made the call again, and we listened.

"I hear something," Lawrence said.

I nodded. "I do, too, and the sound is coming from somewhere between the TV and all those books. Start pulling everything down so we can move this beast."

"Wait," Rue said. "What kind of lowlife drug smuggler reads any books, let alone a Bible? The phone has to be inside it."

Rue's theory made sense. We grabbed the books, gave them a shake, and flipped all the pages for a cutout section but found nothing. I pointed at the Bible.

"It's got to be that one. Defiling a Bible is grounds for incarceration in itself." I pulled the Bible off the shelf, flipped through it, and found nothing. "Well, shit. Call the number again, and everyone come to this side of the cabinet and listen." I didn't want to tackle moving that heavy thing, which probably weighed five hundred pounds, unless absolutely necessary. We gathered between the TV and the end of the cabinet—a five-foot distance—and listened. The vibration was closer to the end. We removed everything from that side, including the items in the lower drawers, but the phone wasn't there.

"What the hell? Pull the drawers completely out of the cabinet. There has to be a hidden compartment or a cutout somewhere."

Lawrence jiggled the drawers until they slid out. He

engaged his phone's flashlight and stuck his head inside the void. "Got it! There's a section of the cabinet's bottom about the size of a shoebox that's cut out. The phone and some papers are inside."

"Good. Don't touch anything until you take a few pictures."

Lawrence did and then, with his gloved hand, passed the cache to us. "Here you go."

I grinned. "Mateo Garcia is in for a rude awakening. That son of a bitch isn't going to know what hit him when he's picked up and extradited to the United States by this time tomorrow."

Chapter 10

It was shift change by the time we'd returned to the station and gathered downstairs in the briefing room we shared with SVU. That was the best-case scenario. After we went through the items we found at Luis's house, Juan Ramirez, one of the SVU officers, would translate everything for the group. Every text message and the notes found with the phone were all written in Spanish. Since both Luis and Mateo were fluent in English, I assumed that was a secondary measure of caution in case those items wound up in the wrong hands—like ours.

According to Ramirez, the notes were likely written by Luis. They included Cynthia's new address, her boyfriend's name and where he lived, and Cynthia's current place of employment—the boyfriend's restaurant. That told me that depending on Mateo's pecking order in the gangs, Daniel and his business might be in danger.

The text message went back only two weeks and only between Mateo and Luis, which was perfect. That meant Mateo would likely respond to every message sent, but it would have to be sent by someone well-versed in Spanish. SVU had several Spanish-speaking officers, but we were dealing with murder, and that took precedence over everything else. I wasn't planning to hand over the phone to them. Beginning that night, we needed someone in our department to send and respond to every text between Luis and Mateo. That person would be in charge of the phone and keep it in their possession, which was another problem all its own. Nobody in our department was of Spanish descent or spoke the language fluently enough to sound absolutely normal without messing up words. We had to come up with something quickly, though, or Mateo would wonder about the hours of silence that had already passed.

"We need something that can translate the messages Mateo sends in the texts and what our response will be," Ricky said.

He was right. That was the only thing that would work. I offered to take the phone to our tech department, talk to Tom Branch about it before he left for the night, and come up with something that would work. Since the phone was a new model, it was likely that a speech translator tool was already built in.

Our tech department was on the same floor—the lower level. All I needed to do was walk the phone down the hallway and make one right-hand turn to reach Tech. It would take only a minute or so.

With Royce's okay, I left the room and took off down the hall. I reached the tech department just as Kyle, the part-time evening technician and weekend warrior, walked in.

"Can I help you with something, Mitch?"

"Yeah, but I need Tom's input too."

"Sure. Come on in."

We found Tom at the back of their department, finishing up a task at one of the many computer stations. Kyle called out to him.

"Mitch needs your expertise on something."

Tom stood and headed our way. "What's up?"

"We found this burner phone at Luis Ortega's house. The communication is only between him and Mateo Garcia."

Tom's eyebrows shot up. "Great find."

"Right, except all of their communication is in Spanish. I need to act like I'm Luis, but I can't read, speak, or spell a damn thing in Spanish."

Tom chuckled. "That's okay. Can I take a look?"

I gladly handed over the phone. "Be my guest."

Tom went into Settings and made a few adjustments. "As long as you don't intend to make a physical call, you should be okay. The program in this phone is kind of like Google Translate. You can highlight his words and have them translated into English or any language available and vice versa. You should be good to go."

I tipped my head with relief. "That's it?"

"Yep. Let me give you an example with Kyle's phone and my own in case you run into a hiccup. Go ahead and type your message in English and then set your speech to Spanish, Kyle." He did, and it changed his words to Spanish.

"Now send the text to my phone."

I watched as Kyle sent it, and Tom received it.

"Okay, take a look, Mitch. The message came to me in Spanish, but I can highlight it and set it to English. See how it just translated Kyle's message into English? Pretty slick, huh?"

"It sure is. I guess that solved my problem. And the language is translated exactly as it's written, in case slang is used too?"

"It should be able to translate anything you type. Just keep the words pretty generic."

"Great. Thanks, guys." I headed back to the group with the good news. Now to see who would keep that phone in their possession. Royce would likely make that decision and then call it a night for us first shift guys. It was time to go home. I was starving, tomorrow was another day, and I was anxious to hear about the communication between Mateo and Luis going forward.

I explained the process then handed the phone to Royce. He waved me off.

"You're keeping it and will be Luis from now on."

"Huh? Me? Tomorrow is my last day of work until next Wednesday. I'll be out of the loop."

"Nope, you'll be smack dab in the center of the loop. You're taking this phone along on your Yucatan Peninsula cruise. Chances are at any given point, you might be within an hour or less of his location. You can swoop in and nab him."

"But he knows my face. He'd recognize me."

Royce swatted away my doubts. "That's why tourists wear wide-brimmed hats and sunglasses. It's that strong sun, you know. Everyone does it, and you'll blend right in. Anyway, the Federales would have to be involved too."

I swallowed hard and wondered how that would go over on my mom's seventieth birthday cruise. It was supposed to be all about her with land excursions and events on the ship. If I was preoccupied with the damn phone, I didn't know how much attention she would actually get.

"But—"

"No buts. All you need to do is keep up communications with Mateo and find out where he is. Stay in constant contact with us by using your personal cell phone, and we'll have that jerk back here and sitting in one of our jail cells before the weekend. Any questions?"

I didn't have a choice and would have to make the best of it. Thank God my mom and I didn't have a shared room. I would be spreading myself thin over the five-day cruise, but at least I'd have tomorrow to practice with the phone before I took it, and my job, along on my mom's birthday vacation.

Chapter 11

I confided in Marie after I got home that night, and she was horrified.

"How can you take work along when it's supposed to be a celebration for Mom? She's wanted to go on a cruise forever."

"And it will be a celebration for Mom. We'll have fun. I promise. Anything I do with that phone and the messages I send and receive shouldn't take but a few minutes every so often."

With a hard sigh, Marie shook her head. "I have my doubts. If this killer's location comes in, you'll have to act on it. You can't hide *that* from Mom. There's a good possibility that anything related to that damn case could ruin Mom's entire five-day trip."

"Sorry, Sis. There's no reason that you or Meg couldn't have gone."

"We have kids who are in school."

"And I have a job that usually runs around the clock. Murderers don't take time off just because I got railroaded into escorting Mom on this trip."

Marie pulled back. "So you've been railroaded?"

It was too late. I couldn't take back my words, and I felt terrible. All I could do was apologize, eat supper, and go to bed. And I hoped for the best—that through text messages from Mateo, we would learn of his location, set the trap, and spring it before I ever took a foot off American soil and placed it on that ship.

At eight thirty, I thanked Marie for the great chicken cacciatore supper and excused myself. I could work in my room with my laptop or phone so the kids could watch their last TV show of the night downstairs with Marie. By nine thirty, the kids were in bed, the downstairs went silent, and I assumed Marie had gone to bed as well.

I'd created a to-do list that included calling my own phone provider and Luis's to make sure both phones had unlimited international service during the five days I was on the ship or on land excursions in Mexico. I reviewed the itinerary again and saw that Saturday, we were scheduled to visit the ruins of Tulum and the sacred cenote pools then enjoy a stroll through the colonial city of Valladolid before returning to the ship for supper. Sunday had already been booked for an afternoon archeological tour on the island of Cozumel. I groaned and hoped for phone reception in those locations if needed. Even though I would physically be on vacation, my thoughts, my eyes, and my ears needed to be at work.

Having Savannah and the Yucatan Peninsula in the same time zone was helpful since I would probably be awake and asleep at the same time as Mateo.

After making sure the burner phone was set at a loud vibrate, I placed it under my pillow, turned off the light, and hoped that by morning, the tense feelings between Marie and me would be gone.

I had no idea how long I'd been sleeping when something vibrated against my left ear. I was dreaming of bees swarming me and instinctively swatted at my head. I woke, felt the same buzzing, and realized it was a text coming in.

"Shit!" I jumped up, fully awake, and twisted the lamp's switch. The room lit up. I grabbed the phone, propped pillows behind my back, and highlighted the text, translated it into English, and read it. Mateo wanted an update on the conditions of Cynthia and the kids. I was between a rock and a hard place and didn't know how to respond. I wasn't given carte blanche to say anything I wanted in those back-and-forth texts, and when the time came that Mateo wanted to actually talk—well, I didn't even want to go there. Hopefully, he would be in custody before that ever happened.

I checked the time—2:04 a.m. I needed to call Royce and wake him up anyway. With a frown, I tapped on his name in my contact list.

"Yeah?" He croaked out the words, which told me he was definitely an open-mouth sleeper.

"Sorry to wake you, Boss, but Mateo just texted me. He wants an update on Cynthia and the kids. What do I tell him? That Cynthia is dead?"

"Shit. Let me think for a minute. I have to take a piss and get a glass of water. I'll call you right back."

Royce hung up, and as I waited, I wondered what the best

response would be. Telling Mateo that Cynthia had died might push him deeper into remote areas, where he might never pop up on our radar. Telling him that they'd all lived through the shootings might also send him deeper into the unknown. They would be able to confirm who their attacker was, even though everyone knew it was Mateo anyway—Luis had practically admitted it. Besides that, people didn't flee to other countries and hide if they'd done nothing wrong. But telling him that the three had lived might make him drop his guard. He could sneak back into the US with intentions of finishing them off for good. There were too many choices to pick from, and making that decision was way above my pay grade.

Three minutes later, my phone rang. We couldn't talk for long—Mateo was likely expecting a response that night. Tomorrow, I would look at all of his and Luis's communications to see when they usually took place, the amount of time that lapsed between them, and how many texts were normally exchanged throughout the day. I needed to expedite Mateo's capture, so that meant pushing him for his location without causing him to become suspicious.

"Hey, Boss, decide what to do?"

"Damn it. I don't know which is the best way to go. I think you'll have to say they're still alive and the doctors are hopeful they'll recover. That could buy us time and keep him from switching up his locations."

"I will if that's what you want me to do. The text came in seven minutes ago, and by the way the back-and-forth messages went between them this morning, they typically respond within minutes. So if that's a for-sure response, I'll send it."

"Um, yeah, and then don't text him any more tonight. If you do, you'll be up all night, and so will I."

I huffed. "Okay. I'll do it now. See you in the morning." I ended the call with Royce, nervously tapped my text response, converted it to Spanish, and hit Send. I hoped Mateo would leave me alone for the rest of the night. I could only see the texting getting tougher as the days went on, especially when I was on my own if I couldn't get through to anyone at the precinct.

I slid the phone under my pillow and wished for morning. I didn't want to deal with him again, and I needed a good night's sleep, but shutting down my mind was another thing altogether.

The next morning, my alarm woke me. I had actually fallen asleep, and after yanking the burner phone out from under my pillow, I saw that no more texts had come in last night, so I hadn't missed any. I was relieved.

I headed downstairs for my first cup of coffee and noticed that Marie wasn't cooking up a storm like she usually was. I groaned.

She's still pissed at me.

Tomorrow, Mom and I would leave Savannah and wouldn't be back until after dark on Tuesday. It would be nice to make peace with Marie before we left. Otherwise, the tension would be noticed by Mom and Meg.

With my coffee in hand, I went upstairs and heard chatter coming from the girls' bedroom. Marie was in there with them, probably getting them up for school. I gave the door a knock and waited.

Seconds later, Della swung open the door, still in her pj's, and asked what I wanted.

"I need to talk to your mama for a second, honey."

Della yelled out, "Mama, Uncle Mitch wants you!"

I grinned when I saw Marie sitting on Della's bed only four feet away. She couldn't hold back her smile at her daughter's goofiness.

"You girls hurry up and get dressed. I need to get downstairs and make breakfast."

Gus waddled downstairs behind us, and I let him out before taking a seat at the breakfast bar.

"Sis—"

"No, *I'm* sorry. You were right. Meg and I did railroad you into going with Mom. At the time, we thought it was funny, but nothing about your job or the commitment you have to it is funny. The job you do protects the rest of us from harm. We shouldn't have been so insensitive."

"Well, thanks, and believe me, I'll do my best to make sure Mom has a great time. Just so you know, her next birthday celebration is on you and Meg."

Marie smiled. "Deal. So what do you want for breakfast?"

I guzzled my coffee, poured another cup, and headed for the stairs. "An English muffin is enough for me. I need to get to work. I have a feeling it's going to be a busy day."

Chapter 12

I arrived at work to an eerily somber setting. Something was definitely wrong. Rue was already in our office when I walked in.

"What the heck is going on? This place is as quiet as a morgue."

He grimaced. Was it my choice of words?

"Francesca and Calen died during the night."

"What? Damn it!" I punched my open hand with my fist, now with even more hatred toward Mateo than I thought possible. I dropped down in my chair. "So, what's going on? What does Royce say?"

"He literally found out fifteen minutes ago and then passed it on to me, Lawrence, and Bentley. The whole station will know soon enough once the joint meeting begins."

"Shit. Has anyone told the grandparents yet?"

Rue shook his head. "Doubt it's gotten that far, buddy, but it's definitely a real shame."

I was beginning to feel the weight of my upcoming task and wondered if I could actually find out Mateo's location or if asking would spook him. If I could find it out, then the

FBI would hopefully take over, swoop in with the Federales, and grab that piece of shit. I needed to speak to Royce about being in charge of that cell phone. Since three people had died, two of them teenagers, I wondered whether the FBI would take over the case immediately or leave it in the hands of one homicide detective who was on a five-day cruise with his mother. That had sounded like a good idea at first, but suddenly, I wasn't so sure, and I would definitely ask that question at the meeting.

"Let's go."

I stared at my hands as I thought about three upcoming funerals. It was too much for any family to bear.

"Cannon?"

I looked up, and Rue was waiting at the door.

"You coming? The meeting is about to start."

"Oh, yeah, sorry. Guess my mind is elsewhere."

We took the stairs down to our lower-level conference room, where thirty or more people were already seated. A low-pitched buzz filled the room until Timmons called for everyone's attention.

"It sounds like you've all heard about the unfortunate deaths of Francesca and Calen Lopez. As the sergeant in SVU, I can say our department is out of the game, but as a father and fellow officer, I want the homicide division to know we're in it to stay in it until Mateo Garcia has been captured and is back on US soil. Any help we can lend, we're there. Just say the word."

We sat silently as Royce took the podium. He unfolded a sheet of paper, likely his bullet-pointed updates. There would be time for all of our questions at the end of the meeting.

He coughed into his fist, took a drink of water, and began. "First, I want to update everyone on Mateo's car, not that it matters now, but the BOLO was pulled on it. Patrol found it in the lot of an apartment building seven blocks from the airport. It's been taken to the crime lab for a good going through. Also, I spoke with a supervisory agent at Savannah's FBI field office this morning. The local branch is familiar with Mateo Garcia's name and is aware of the latest news. At this moment in time, Garcia isn't listed as an FBI fugitive since he isn't on their watch list yet. His crimes are too recent—only a few days old—and there's another situation going on with the political side of the coin. Prisoners' rights groups have made a big impact recently, and—" Royce wiped his brow. "Well, I don't have to tell you about all the defunding nonsense and the release of prisoners who should never see the light of day, all due to overcrowding in the prison system as a whole. Lightweights usually get out first and murderers go last, but drug smugglers sit somewhere in that gray area. Unfortunately, nobody knew how dangerous and volatile Mateo was until after his release, and that's the way it usually turns out. The criminal gets a pass, and the innocent people get injured or killed." He groaned. "I know, I'm rambling. To make a long story short, they aren't quite ready to go after Garcia yet. The FBI Fugitive Task Force isn't involved, and they don't intend to be until he's considered a fugitive in accordance with their description of it." Royce held up his hands when he saw protests coming his way. "Hang on, hang on. We'll get to the questions at the end. Now, since SVU is willing to pitch in, I'd like to have that department see what they can do to protect Mr. Ruiz and his business. There may be threats coming his way. Mateo has a wide web of friends and acquaintances in the south, and we need those criminals to remain at arm's length." He turned to Timmons. "Possibly a task force involving SVU and Vice. Find the worst offenders and gang members and dig them out of the holes they're hiding in."

"Consider it done," Timmons said.

Royce continued. "The prison system needs to take some heat on this, and I'll personally speak with Warden Myer about the decision to release Mateo and what their parameters are in making those decisions. The prisons need reform but reform to protect the innocent from the monsters who should remain behind bars indefinitely."

I looked from side to side, and my fellow officers were nodding.

Royce scanned the room. "Okay, let's have some questions. You've got twenty minutes since we have a department to run and a city to protect."

Rue spoke up. "Luis needs to be talked to again before Mitch is out and on his own for the next few days."

Royce rolled his neck as he listened. "Luis won't talk, and his slimy public defender will make sure he doesn't. We can try for a deal, but he'd have to give us something worthwhile today. Lawrence and Bentley can get on that as soon as we're done here."

I knew everyone was waiting for me to say something, so I sucked in a deep breath and took my turn. "Is this really going to work as far as me pretending to be Luis?"

"Did Mateo contact you again last night after the text he sent?"

I tipped my head and had to admit that he hadn't.

"As long as you don't say too much, he'll believe you're Luis. Take some time today and review every text exchanged between them on that burner. Convert every message to English and study how Luis talks. Be him. It's the only way to track down Mateo. You and Rue can practice on your own phones so it's second nature to you."

I had to do my part and couldn't back out simply because the timing sucked. I would make it up to my mom one way or another, even if it meant while on the ship, I played bingo and did water aerobics with her.

"So what's the plan if he does disclose his location? He can't just say something generic like he's in Mexico. We'd need an exact location in order to scoop him up."

Royce agreed and scratched his cheek. "And that's where you work your magic, Cannon. Fool that son of a bitch into thinking you're his best friend however you can. You'll get the location out of him one way or another."

Chapter 13

Marie called me twice while I was at work. She wanted to know how many suitcases would fit in my Corvette.

"Why?"

"Because Mom says she needs to take two. One for casual clothes and one with her nicer outfits for the ship dinners."

I groaned knowing full well that I would be taking three changes of clothes and Mom would be taking ten. "My car can't hold more than two suitcases unless you want to swap cars for five full days and have seven hundred more miles put on your Accord. There's also the fact that my car only has two seats. Would one of the kids ride in the trunk if you had to go somewhere?"

"Mitch!"

"You know I'm kidding, Sis, but Mom gets one suitcase and a beach bag or backpack. That's it. I'm not wearing the same two or three outfits from Thursday until the following Tuesday night. Make it work."

"Okay, okay. I'll tell her. Is there room for souvenirs?"

"If they fit in her bag, yes. Otherwise, no."

"All right. I'll leave you alone to finish up your workday. Don't be late for supper."

"Yes, ma'am." I hung up with a grunt.

Rue chuckled. "Is having your sister live with you everything you thought it would be?"

I huffed. "Yeah, and more. I'm joking of course. Marie is great, but sometimes, I feel like she and Mom are the same person."

"That's because she's the oldest and second in charge to your mom."

"You're probably right. I just want this *vacation* to be in the rearview mirror so I can get back to my normal routine."

"Okay, let's go over Luis's way of talking again."

I pulled up the screenshot of the text messages we'd converted to English and printed out. Luckily, Luis didn't use a lot of slang words. He spoke in everyday language, which would make it easier for me to impersonate him.

By lunchtime, we had the texting conversations down pat. I was again confident that I could pull off the ruse and somehow, someway, find out where Mateo was holed up. I just needed to make sure the few people I would have to contact while I was physically cruising around the Yucatan Peninsula had their phones handy every second of every day.

Lawrence and Bentley returned from their meeting with Luis and his attorney. They said they'd gotten nowhere with the two, and no deals were made. According to the lawyer, we were bluffing, and it meant nothing that Luis had kept Mateo updated about Cynthia through letters and calls to the prison. Those acts had nothing to do with Mateo's eventual actions. The blame would be put on the prison system for releasing him. Luis intended to take his chances in court and would definitely be exonerated.

"Damn it. I guess it's on me again to find that slimeball." I glanced at the clock—1:19. I had four more hours before leaving the station until next Wednesday, and the team was counting on me to find Mateo. Doubt still filled my mind and weighed heavily on my shoulders, but in the long run, if I didn't find Mateo, he'd still be captured someday by the FBI or the local police wherever he might be.

I reached across my desk and called Royce. "Hey, Boss, has anyone updated Mr. and Mrs. Lopez about Francesca and Calen?"

"Yeah, they were notified this morning by the hospital since they're on the family list. I should send somebody to their hotel to offer our condolences, though. It's the proper thing to do."

"How about Rue and I take care of that since we had the initial contact with them anyway?"

"Sure. Go ahead."

It was two o'clock by the time we reached the hotel. I had to admit that Welcome Inn was a catchy name for a hotel, but I didn't have the welcoming feel at that moment like the name implied. I knew Mr. and Mrs. Lopez were aware of the deaths and that we were just stopping by to offer our condolences and answer any more questions they might have, but it didn't make things easier.

We knocked on their door, and Dina allowed us in.

"We already were informed of the news this morning, Detectives," she said as she started a four-cup pot of coffee.

We took seats at the round table that sat in the corner of

the room. The window in front of us overlooked the distant airport. My mind drifted for a second, and I wondered whether Jeff, my brother-in-law, was up in the tower, directing planes in and out that day.

Rue began, and his words brought me back to the present. "Dina, Joe, you have our deepest condolences. The passing of Cynthia and the kids has to be the hardest challenge you've ever gone through, and I assure you we're doing our best to track down Mateo. Right now, those words may sound hollow, but once he's locked up for life or sits on death row, I'm sure you'll get a certain amount of satisfaction from it."

Joe shook his head. "I have my doubts, Detective Rue. He was locked up, our daughter and grandkids were safe, but now they're dead just because of some bullshit prison board decision. I'm going to sue them. That's for sure."

I spoke up. "And legally, you have every right to do that. I can't tell you what to expect for an outcome, and only an attorney can help you with that, but rest assured, our sergeant will be talking to the warden about the situation."

"Too little too late," Dina said. "When can we give our family a proper burial, and who's going to pay for it, us or the prison for releasing him to kill our children?"

I shook my head. "I don't have those answers, ma'am, but a good attorney will."

"We're going back to Atlanta on Saturday. Will our loved ones be going then too? Why do the police need to hold on to their bodies?"

"I'll check into that and let you know before the end of the day, sir," I said.

Joe stood, filled the coffee cups, and paced with his.

I couldn't tell them much, but I could try to ease their pain. "Over the weekend, I'm going to do my best to track down Mateo. We think he's somewhere south of the border, but we don't have his exact location pinned down yet. If anything changes, we'll certainly let you know."

"We'd appreciate that, Detective Cannon."

We finished our coffee, thanked Dina for making it, and left our cards with the couple. The devastation showed on their faces, and I couldn't imagine the pain they were going through, but I would do my best to bring Mateo to justice.

We made a stop at Royce's office on our way back to ours. I had something to run by him.

"Hey, Boss, got a sec?"

"Yep, shoot."

"Do you think it would help or hinder catching Mateo if we aired his photo and likely whereabouts on one of those international fugitive shows?"

Royce ran both hands through his thinning hair. "We discussed that before, Mitch."

"But that was when he was on the hook for one murder, not three. Maybe those TV shows would see the urgency in capturing him now."

"Right, but we don't want to give him a heads-up that we're coming after him. Let him think his whereabouts are unknown."

Rue wrinkled his forehead. "Last I heard, his whereabouts *were* unknown."

"True, but I have faith in Cannon. He'll dig that rat out

of his hole. Let's try that first. If we don't have Mateo in custody by the time Mitch is back on terra firma, we'll go all out guns blazing to make an arrest."

I didn't feel as confident as Royce and wondered why we couldn't just go all out guns blazing now. I had two hours of work remaining before I left and was on my own. No matter what, I would give the next five days everything I had.

Chapter 14

It was time. My workday had ended, a few loose ends had been tied up, and Mateo Garcia was still in the wind. None of our contacts from south of the border said he'd been seen or spoken to any of their informants, and in a few minutes, I would be on my own with nothing but a burner phone, my mom, and soon enough, a ship out in the ocean to fill my time. I was waiting for that moment to rear its ugly head when I would have to think of an excuse for why I couldn't talk to Mateo over the phone. I had to come up with a believable story, and that night, I would write down some scenarios and excuses and keep them handy at all times.

I said goodbye to my day and night shift team, went over a few necessary what-ifs with Royce, and wrote down critical phone numbers in Mexico, Guatemala, and Belize in case I needed them.

With a pat on my shoulder, Rue said goodbye and wished me luck with Mateo and even more luck with my mom. He chuckled, said he'd see me soon, and reminded me not to drink the tap water.

With slumped shoulders, I walked out, and even though

the case had been handed to me to do with what I could, I somehow felt out of the loop. Before driving away, I checked the burner phone. Nothing new had come in. I wondered if Mateo was just lying low or if he was on the move. I would make contact later that night, hope for a response, and pray that he didn't try to reach me during my drive to Tampa.

I arrived home at 5:40 and was surprised to see my mom there. I was hoping for one last night to myself before she talked my ear off during the drive tomorrow. Maybe I could slip chamomile tea into a travel mug for her in the morning.

I walked in to a cheerful house and felt a twinge of guilt. I needed to lighten up. It wasn't my job to take down the killer single-handedly. I would do my best to find his location then enjoy my mom's seventieth-birthday cruise.

"Hey, guys." I cracked the best smile I could muster up.

"Hey, honey." My mom tapped her cheek. That meant I needed to cross the room, bend down, and kiss that spot, so I did.

"Hi, Mom. How ya doing? Did you figure out your wardrobe for the next few days?"

She gave me a stern look. "I brought two suitcases. You need to make them fit in that go-cart of yours."

I glanced at Marie, who shrugged and headed to the kitchen with her palms up. "Supper will be ready in ten minutes," she said as she left the scene.

The girls were reading a story to my mom, so I took that opportunity to follow Marie into the kitchen. "What the hell, Sis?"

"Don't even start. I told her one suitcase, but she said it

was her vacation and she wanted to look good. What was I supposed to say?"

I sighed and wondered if it was just the beginning of a really bad idea. "Next time—"

"There isn't going to be a next time, bro. If Mom wants to do another cruise, I'll set it up with a senior single ladies tour and drive her to the damn ship myself. That way, she can take six suitcases if she wants."

"Good." I pointed at her and gave her the stink eye. "I'm not forgetting this conversation."

"Who knows? Maybe you'll have fun," she said with half a grin.

"Right. What's for supper? Anything I like?" I walked to the stove, used the hot pad to lift the lid on the simmering pot, and took a sniff. "Mmmm… homemade spaghetti sauce. Meatballs in the oven?"

"Of course." She swatted me with the dish towel as I walked by. "Now go wash up." Marie yelled into the living room. "Girls, get in here and set the table!"

Mom talked nonstop during dinner. I caught Della rolling her eyes and elbowing Chloe on several occasions. I gave her a stern look.

"Grandma, what are you and Uncle Mitch going to do on the ship?" Della asked.

Mom chuckled. "Not sure yet, honey. I have no idea what kind of activities they offer. Guess we'll see when we see. I'd love to play shuffleboard, though, and take a dip or two in their pool."

"Uncle Mitch, do they have pool slides like they show on TV?"

I grinned at Della. "Maybe, kiddo, but I think you two should come along to keep Grandma company."

They bounced up and down on their chairs. "Can we go, Mama?"

"Of course not. It's too late to include you two, and you both have school."

Della frowned. "So, why did you say that, Uncle Mitch?"

I shrugged. "Because I just might belly up to the bar. It's all inclusive, you know."

Della and Chloe laughed, and Mom gave me the stink eye. "Don't mind him, girls. He's pulling your leg. We'll have loads of fun. I can just feel it."

Marie gave me a wink, and I gave her my best snarl. I couldn't wait for Tuesday to arrive.

I told Mom we were leaving at nine thirty in the morning. We would have a good breakfast, load the car, fill it with gas, and be on our way. I said good night and turned in at ten o'clock.

With my bedroom door closed for privacy, I grabbed the burner phone and sent a text to Mateo, hoping for a response before I fell asleep. I asked if he was hunkered down in a good spot where he could stay or if moving to another location made more sense. With any luck, he might say what area he was holed up in, then I could push a little harder. I had a plan in mind that just might work. After fifteen minutes of waiting, I was getting drowsy. I set the vibration to its highest setting, put the phone under my pillow, and shut off the light. Surely, I would feel it if a response came in.

I woke to the sound of the kids running through the

hallway. I cracked open my eyes, and it was light outside. "Shit, did I miss a text?" I yanked the phone from under my pillow, and a message alert was showing. That unnerved me. How was I going to correspond with Mateo if I slept through a text coming in?

Calm down. I'll be in my own room on the ship. Mom won't know if I get a text at night or not.

I reminded myself to set the burner to vibrate during the day then switch it to the sound mode once I was alone for the night.

I tapped the text I'd missed and converted it to English. It was short and to the point. Mateo mentioned that he was almost out of minutes since he'd been using the phone with his local contacts too. That information would only strengthen my plan. He said he was in Quintana Roo, but that was a large area to search. At least I knew he was in Mexico.

Chapter 15

After breakfast with the kids and Marie, Mom and I said goodbye and watched out the window as Marie walked Chloe and Della to the bus stop at the end of the block.

"I guess I'll get showered and dressed," Mom said.

"Good plan. We need to leave in an hour."

I waited until she'd gone upstairs and I heard the shower running before I called Royce. It would probably be my only call before reaching Tampa.

"Hey, Boss, I wanted to run something by you before Marie or my mom hear me talking shop."

"Sure, go ahead."

"Mateo told me he's in Quintana Roo but didn't say where. He said he was running low on minutes since he was using that phone with his contacts south of the border too."

"Okay. What do you have in mind?"

"Not quite sure, but if someone at the precinct can come up with a location like a mail drop or a place in Quintana Roo where Mateo can pick up something, maybe we can nab him there."

"Hmm... like a money transfer store? Wire cash for him

to buy a new phone there that has unlimited minutes?"

"Yeah, something like that. He's probably getting short on cash anyway. It isn't like he was released from prison with a boatload of money. Luis bought his plane ticket, but I can't see him fronting Mateo a thousand bucks. I could tell him to go to XYZ store, the one you pick out, sign for the cash, then get a better burner phone with unlimited minutes and send Luis the number. That kind of thing always trips up the crook, especially when cash is mentioned."

"Okay, I like it. I'll text you a location later, and when you talk to him, ask if he's anywhere near there. If he is, then we'll go ahead with the plan. Have fun with your mom. When are you heading out?"

"Soon. Within the hour. It should be an adventure, I'm sure."

Royce chuckled and hung up. Maybe later that day, we could begin setting the rat trap.

"All done and dressed."

"That's good, Mom. Are your suitcases ready to put in the car?"

"Yep, and you can go up and get them."

Marie walked in and heard the end of the conversation. "Go ahead and get ready, bro. I'll bring Mom's suitcases down."

I nodded a thanks and went upstairs to shower.

Forty minutes later and with the car jam packed, Mom ran through her "to bring" list for the third time. Meg popped in to see us off. I could tell by the expressions both my sisters wore that they still thought the entire trip was funny. I knew it was payback for being the youngest child since I'd always had Mom wrapped around my little finger and gotten away with murder.

After kisses and hugs were shared, I finally got Mom into my Corvette as she complained about how low to the ground it was and how she would never be able to get out of it. I glared at Meg and Marie while they did their best to hold back laughter.

I settled in behind the wheel, asked Mom if she had her travel mug of tea, and gave Marie a thank-you wink for making it. We were off to the gas station. After that, we would jump on I-95 South until we reached Jacksonville, Florida, then cut west to I-10 and stay on that until we reached I-75, then head south again. Just west of Wesley Chapel, we would cut off onto I-275 and that would take us right into Tampa. I planned to stop in Jacksonville for lunch then make it to Tampa by late afternoon. Marie had already booked us a hotel for the night, located only minutes from the cruise ship. After our arrival in Tampa, there was a chance that my mood would improve. From what I had looked up online, the Channel District and Sparkman Wharf were beautiful at night. Mom would enjoy walking the area and grabbing supper at one of the outdoor restaurants.

We were off. After fueling up, I merged onto I-95 heading south. I wondered what Mom and I would talk about or whether she would stare out the window as the hours passed. I'd let her lead—either we'd remain quiet, she'd sleep, or we'd pick up a conversation since it wasn't often that we were alone together.

Hours passed without much talking between us. I glanced at my mom every now and then and hoped the silence was because she'd dozed off, but she hadn't.

We were only fifty miles north of Jacksonville, and so far, our conversations were mostly about Marie's upcoming divorce court date and whether she and the girls enjoyed living in the family home again. I responded with what I knew, but I was sure they were conversations Marie had already shared with Mom. I knew she was making small talk to fill what could be an awkward silence. The thought made me wonder how long it had been since Mom and I hung out together without any other family members around. Likely not since she'd moved into the active senior campus, and that was several years back.

I was slipping, and as the only male in our family, I wasn't doing my part to be present with my loved ones. I relied too much on my sisters to entertain our mom while I dug deeper and deeper into my work. I needed to step up—family was everything, I'd always said—and I had to prove I meant it. I had to come clean with my mom and be honest with her. I had to let her know that this was a working vacation for me.

"Mom?"

She faced me. "I know you didn't want to go on this trip, Mitch. I heard you and Marie talking last night."

I felt horrible all over again. "I'm so sorry. My reasoning is mostly work-related, and I guess I thought you'd enjoy the company of Marie or Meg more than me. I mean, what do we have in common anyway?"

She smiled. "We're family. Isn't that enough? We need to

reconnect. My kids are my kids. I have no preference whether you're male or female. I love you all the same."

My words stuck in my throat. I needed to fix the situation and let Mom know that the five-day trip wasn't a burden but, instead, a good way for us to reconnect. I coughed into my fist then began.

"Honestly, I thought you'd have more fun with Marie or Meg, and admittedly, I was angry when they sprung the trip on me. I wasn't part of the planning."

"Well, that's just rude."

I smiled. My mom didn't mince words.

"Anyway, I accepted it. After all, it is your seventieth birthday, and that's a big deal. Marie and Meg meant well, but the kids are in school, and I have a lot of vacation time built up. Then, a particular prisoner I'm familiar with was released due to overcrowding."

Mom swatted the air. "That isn't right. If you don't want to do the time, then don't commit the crime. Otherwise, deal with it."

I grinned again. My outspoken mom was saying her piece.

"The worst part is, after he was released, he shot his ex-girlfriend and her two kids. I don't often talk about my cases with you, but I think I have some explaining to do."

Mom looked at me with horror written across her face. "Tell me they made it."

"If only they were that lucky. Catching that maniac almost feels personal to me. He should never have seen the light of day, and that's on the prison board."

"I should think so. Are there any leads to his whereabouts?

That man needs to sit on death row."

I steeled myself. "We located a burner phone that his buddy Luis Ortega bought to communicate with Mateo. We interviewed Luis, and he's being held in jail right now for facilitating Mateo's passage out of the country."

"Out of the country? So where is he?"

I groaned. "We're pretty sure he's hiding out in Quintana Roo."

"Where on earth is that?"

"It's in Mexico, Mom."

"Oh, hell no. Don't even go there."

Chapter 16

If eye daggers could kill, I would have been dead the minute the word *Mexico* came out of my mouth.

My mom didn't say another word to me until we stopped for lunch at a restaurant along the interstate, just outside Jacksonville. There, she told me she was going to the ladies' room, and that wasn't actually talking to me either.

I was shown to a booth and ordered two coffees while I waited for her to join me. After I'd downed half my cup, she finally headed my way and slid into her side of the booth.

I groaned. "Mom."

She held up her hand, and her palm faced me. "I'm angry, and I'm not ready to talk to you yet. I thought this would be our time to really enjoy a mother-and-son relationship, but instead, I'll be doing water aerobics with a bunch of strangers while you're galivanting through Mexico looking for that murderer."

Eyes shot our way, and heads spun.

I leaned forward. "Please keep it down, Mom. People are staring at us."

She snarled. "Let them stare. You're just like your father, Mitch Cannon."

I didn't know whether to take that as a compliment or an insult. "Thanks, I think."

"Don't thank me. He was bullheaded, and everything had to be his way. The apple didn't fall far from the tree if you ask me."

I whispered across the table. "I promise I won't let you down. We're going to enjoy these five days come hell or high water. I can't help it that Mateo Garcia fled the country. It's not like I planned it to happen."

"Then why did you decide to follow up on him? There's how many detectives in Homicide?"

"Enough."

"Exactly."

I watched as Mom's eyes darted toward the waitress heading our way. I held my finger to my lips. "Please don't say anything else until she takes our order and leaves."

The smiling waitress pulled out her order pad. "You folks ready to order?"

I held my breath as Mom began. She often told total strangers her life story, and I hoped she wouldn't do so again just to spite me.

"I'll have the grilled ham-and-cheese with waffle fries and a glass of water." She gave the waitress her best smile then glared at me.

I rolled my eyes. "And I'll have the spinach pie with a side salad. Water too."

"You got it, hon. Waters now?"

"Yes, please." I waited until she was out of earshot before continuing the conversation. "Mom, the only reason I'm point on the Mateo search is because I'll be in the area. I actually have his best friend's burner phone, and I'm pretending to be him. It's the only way to narrow down his location, and then I can let the Federales catch him. We can extradite him to the US as soon as all the papers are signed, and I won't have to be personally involved. All I need to do is communicate with him over the phone once in a while. Can you give me that a few times a day? The rest of our trip will be doing whatever you want to do."

"You promise?"

"Yes, I promise."

A faint smile crossed her lips. I was forgiven, the cat was out of the bag, and I didn't have to hide anything from her anymore. Our trip would go forward without any hard feelings. After sharing what I had to when I needed to make or respond to a text, the rest of the day could be all about her.

We enjoyed our lunch and continued on. We still had a three-hour drive before reaching Tampa. I explained to Mom what the wharf area was like and asked if she wanted to check it out that night and have supper overlooking the water. She was back to normal and seemed enthusiastic about it.

"That would be great, honey, and I can't wait. I've never been to Tampa in my life."

"Well, I never have either, so that's one thing we have in common. Mind if I put on the radio?"

"No, as long as it isn't loud."

I smiled. "It won't be."

Within minutes, my mom was sound asleep. I imagined having a full stomach and a promise from me helped.

While I had time to myself, I thought about the money drop Royce and I had talked about. I wondered if Mateo would actually show up or send somebody to pick up the package in his place. And how would I know when he or someone else would be there? I doubted that the Federales would just sit on a store for hours or days when Mateo hadn't committed any crimes that they knew of in their country. I thought of other scenarios that could work, like putting a tracker on his phone, but that wasn't possible, and it didn't solve his problem of running short on minutes. I needed to talk to Royce, and now I had a better idea. We could buy two new phones with unlimited minutes, have Tech put a tracking app on Mateo's phone under the guise of something else, and send it to one of those stores, where he could pick it up. I would make up some excuse that the cops were snooping around too much and I'd felt the need to get a new burner. I'd send him a companion one with unlimited minutes and data, and it would be more reliable than whatever he found in a mom-and-pop corner store in Mexico. I glanced at my mom again, turned down the radio, and listened to her breathing—slow and regular. She wasn't faking sleep so I made the call to Royce.

"Hey, Boss," I said as soon as he answered. It sounded like he had a mouthful of something—lunch, I assumed.

"What's the word?"

"Nothing. Just got back on the road after lunch. Mom is napping, so I thought I'd run something by you."

"Hang on."

I heard Royce cough, swallow hard, then return to the phone.

"You okay?"

"Yeah, damn sourdough bread is so dry. Got caught in my throat, and I had to wash it down with my iced tea." He coughed again. "So, what were you thinking?"

"Not sure about wiring money to Mateo. If he's off the grid, it could take some time for him to find a reliable place to buy a new cell phone with unlimited data and minutes. What if, as Luis, I say that the cops are sniffing around and I'm afraid they'll find my burner. I'll buy two new phones with unlimited everything and send him one."

"What will that solve?"

"Plenty, if Tech is able to discreetly put a tracking device on it."

"Damn, Cannon, I knew there was a good reason you're my lead detective. I'll get on that right now. You plant the seed, tell Mateo the cops are bugging you, and then tell him you're going to delete all texts between you just in case they find the burner. He'll have a new phone by tomorrow as long as he's able to get to the location you chose to pick it up."

"Great. I'll text him later. No matter what, he knows he can go to Luis if he needs cash. He's not going to stop communicating with him. He'll pick up the phone."

I hung up with thoughts of capturing Mateo and being able to enjoy the vacation with my mom. Everything would work out. I knew it would. It had to.

Chapter 17

Mom woke just as we veered southwest on I-275. She sat up, yawned, and asked where we were.

"We've got about forty-five minutes to go unless we hit a traffic jam."

"I've been sleeping that long? What time is it?"

I tipped my wrist. "It's ten after four. We'll check into the hotel, freshen up, and then take a stroll through the Channelside area if you'd like. I hear it's really nice, and we can use a little exercise after this long car ride. Later, we'll find a good restaurant for supper overlooking the water."

"That sounds wonderful. I'm up for some adventure. Aren't you, Mitch?"

"Sure am, and I bet we'll have some great adventures during our land excursions."

Mom looked genuinely happy again. "I can't wait. I'm so excited."

I grinned. As long as the plan Royce and I had made went without a hitch, I'd be pretty excited too.

A little after five, we reached the Bayview Boutique Hotel, a beautiful place. There wasn't much in the area that looked historic like Savannah, but I was fine with that. High-rise glass-and-steel condos, views of the bay, and swaying palm trees were a nice change of pace. I was ready to relax, take a few mental health days—even if they were with my mom—and enjoy our time together.

I pulled in under the hotel's portico and had our bags loaded onto a brass cart. The attendant followed us to the reservations counter, where I said I could take it from there, then I handed him a tip. We checked in—both rooms faced the water, I was told, which was a plus—then we made our way to the third floor.

"How much time do you need, Mom?"

"Give me twenty minutes. I'll be ready by then."

I carried her bags into her room, made sure it was satisfactory for her, then went to my adjoining room. I washed up, took a peek outside from the small balcony, and liked the view.

Damn, I could get used to taking vacations now and then. Too bad I don't have anyone to share them with, though.

I had just enough time to send Mateo that message about the cops becoming interested in me. I asked what his nearest town was and said I'd send a new cell phone with unlimited data and minutes to a location there. If he needed more cash, I'd send that too. Minutes later, a text came back. Mateo said he and a few others were in Chetumal but were heading north tomorrow. He would update me when he knew more.

"Damn it." I fired off an update to Royce, told him to have the cell phones ready, and as soon as I knew Mateo's location for tomorrow, I'd let him know. They would have to overnight the phone to the nearest pickup location.

It was time to go. I locked up, knocked on my mom's door, and asked if she was ready. She was, and I was determined to do my best to be present and enjoy our night.

We headed to the Riverwalk, which ran alongside the Hillsborough River. From our hotel, it was only a block away. My research had told me that the entire Riverwalk encompassed two and a half miles, farther than I wanted my seventy-year-old mom to go. We would settle for a mile, enjoy the sights, stop for a beverage, then find a nice restaurant for our evening meal. That meant heading east, toward Sparkman Wharf, which was right by the cruise ship terminal. I wanted to see if a parking facility was nearby or if we should take a rideshare tomorrow and leave my car in the private parking garage at the hotel. I decided on the rideshare.

We browsed the shops, stopped for a beer, and continued on to Max's Prime Steakhouse along the waterfront. Mom liked my suggestion that she choose our supper restaurant, and she picked a great one.

We had been seated for only ten minutes when the burner phone buzzed in my pocket. I excused myself to the men's room, but before I did, I asked Mom to choose a bottle of wine to go with our meal. I knew that would occupy her.

In the restroom, I highlighted Mateo's text and translated it to English. He said they would be in Tulum tomorrow, and the next day, they would continue to Puerto Morelos and hunker down for a while. It was a small town off everyone's radar, and he had drug connections there.

"Bingo. That's absolutely perfect." I fired back a message

promising to send the phone and five hundred dollars to a store there. I would locate one on my laptop. I hit Send, and the message was on its way. One quick text to let Royce know and I would be uninterrupted for the rest of the night. I typed the text, reminded him of the cruise ship's name and my cabin number in case there was a blip in cell reception while we were out to sea, and said he should inform the Federales that Mateo Garcia, a drug smuggler who'd fled the US and was responsible for three murders, would be in Puerto Morelos on Saturday. I sent the text on its way and returned to the table, where my mom had already picked out a great bottle of sauvignon blanc.

We enjoyed fresh mahi-mahi, grouper, and a variety platter of shellfish. For dessert, we decided on the crème brulee.

I was happy for the one-mile walk back to our hotel. I was stuffed. The ship would set sail at ten a.m., and before retiring to our rooms, I wanted to ask about a rideshare.

At the concierge desk, I was told that if I signed up that night, we would be shuttled to the ship terminal at no charge, and for fifty dollars, I could leave my car parked at the hotel until Tuesday. I jumped on the deal. I asked Mom if she wanted one more glass of wine at the bar or if she was ready to call it a night. It was pushing nine o'clock.

"One more glass and then I'm done. I think I'll sleep really good tonight."

"Okay, we'll have a light breakfast before we head out. I'll knock on your door at eight fifteen, so be ready."

"Sounds good to me."

Chapter 18

I said good night to my mom at nine forty-five and was sure she would be asleep by ten. Then I went to my room, already tired from the long drive, and checked my phone. No return messages from anyone. Tomorrow, I would call Royce and find out if they'd gotten the new burners. As far as Mateo, I doubted that I'd get many more messages from him. If his phone was almost out of minutes, he would use it sparingly and wait for me to let him know where on Saturday to pick up his new cell phone and the cash. From my phone, I pulled up a map of Mexico to see where Puerto Morelos was—north of Cozumel. We'd literally be passing the town in the cruise ship.

I set my phone's alarm for seven thirty and hoped to fall asleep quickly. Tomorrow was going to be a busy day, and once we were on the ship and situated in our cabins, I would reach out to Royce and Mateo.

I was thankful for the comfortable bed and perfectly squishable pillows and dozed off immediately.

The next morning, the sun pierced my eyelids through the sliver of curtain that wasn't drawn. My alarm had gone off, but I was enjoying a few extra minutes in bed. I reached for my phone, and no return texts had come in from Royce or Mateo. Having forty-five minutes to myself before meeting up with my mom, I started the coffeemaker and hit the shower.

Once fully awake, showered, dressed for the day, and on my second cup of coffee, I tapped Mom's name on my phone and waited as it rang. She picked up a few seconds later.

"Ready to head out, Mom?"

"Good morning, honey, and yes, all packed and ready to go."

"Great. I'll be there in a sec." I hung up, grabbed my packed suitcase, stepped out into the hallway, and knocked on her door.

My eyes bulged when Mom answered dressed in perfect cruise ship attire. Tan knee-length shorts and a bright floral blouse with even brighter pink sandals told me she was dead serious about cruising. She carried a wide-brimmed tan floppy hat to use once we were on the ship, and large dark sunglasses were perched on top of her head.

"Wow, you're making quite the statement."

She smiled. "You like?"

"Definitely. I see now why you wanted to go clothes shopping. You look like a cruise ship pro."

"Thanks, honey. Shall we?"

We headed to the dining room with about forty minutes to go before the hotel's shuttle took us to the cruise ship terminal. A light breakfast was all we needed since the second we stepped foot on the ship, everything we ate and drank would be all-inclusive.

I'd never been on a cruise ship before, but now that we were about to embark, I looked forward to it. Since we'd aired our feelings yesterday and gotten over our disagreements, Mom hadn't done anything to upset me, and hopefully, I hadn't done anything to upset her. Our walk and dinner last night was nice, and the half hour we'd been together so far that morning was going without a hitch.

"Don't order much, Mom. We're leaving on the shuttle in just over a half hour."

"I'm fine with an English muffin and a side of bacon."

"That sounds great." I waved down the waiter and ordered two of the same, along with orange juice and coffee for both of us.

By nine thirty, we had boarded the shuttle for the five-minute ride to the terminal. Once there, I found the customer service desk, showed the smiling woman behind the counter our tickets, and asked where to go. She said we should follow the yellow line out to the dock and check in with the boarding steward. After that, we'd be directed to the check-in counter where we would get our room key cards and a map indicating where our rooms were located.

"That doesn't sound too hard. Are you able to carry one suitcase, Mom? I'll get the other two and your beach bag."

"I'll try. I think I overpacked."

"Here, carry the lightest one. I'll get the rest."

Inside, we stood in line to check in with about thirty people ahead of us. I should have known to come earlier, but we would make the best of it. While Mom went to find the nearest ladies' room, I checked for messages and didn't see any. I made a quick call to Marie and updated her, saying that we'd just boarded the ship but hadn't gotten our room keys yet.

"How's Mom doing?"

"She seems fine after giving me the cold shoulder for a while yesterday. I apologized, came clean with her, and promised that this cruise would be one for the books. Since then, she's been fine."

"Well, you know how Mom gets."

I laughed. "Really? I live with her daughter, remember? You two are one and the same. Speaking of Mom, here she comes."

"Okay, let me talk to her for a minute."

I passed my phone to Mom, who found a chair to sit on while I remained in line. That time could have been a good opportunity to call Royce, but Mom had my phone. Soon, I was only ten people back.

Chapter 19

"What the hell is this?" As he sat in the shaded outdoor courtyard to avoid the morning sun, Mateo read the last text that had come in from Luis. "What? I can't make sense out of this. Has the man gone loco?"

He read the text a half-dozen times before it clicked. It was the only thing that made sense. Luis didn't have the other burner phone at all, and Mateo had no clue how long Detective Cannon had been impersonating him. Last night, an accidental text had come in, one meant for the homicide sergeant, Raleigh Royce, sent by Mitch Cannon, the detective Mateo had had run-ins with in the past. Mateo knew the man well.

Before he'd shut down the phone last night, Mateo read the previous message, which he'd thought Luis had sent. It stated that a new phone with unlimited minutes and data, along with five hundred dollars, would be sent to a drop-off store in Puerto Morelos on Saturday. Luis would find a store and send Mateo the address. The very next message—the one that Mateo had just discovered—was supposed to have been sent to Royce. That one read that Mateo would be in Tulum on Friday and Puerto Morelos, where he planned to hunker down, on Saturday. The town was small and off everyone's radar, and he had drug connections there. The text also said to contact the Federales since Mateo was a drug smuggler who had killed three people and fled south. Cannon mentioned the name of the cruise ship that he and his mother were on, as well as his stateroom number, in case the cell service was sketchy.

So that son of a bitch has been playing me all along? If he has Luis's burner phone, then that means Luis is in jail. Otherwise, he would have warned me. The question is, how do I get back at Cannon in spades and show him a Mexican vacation that came straight out of hell? The only way I know is through his mama.

Mateo called out to his allies. "I need to know when the *Evening Star Princess* is set to reach Playa del Carmen tomorrow. I want to know if Detective Mitch Cannon and his mother are signed up for any land excursions too. He's staying in stateroom 319. I don't care how you find out. Just do it and do it now! I'll show that son of a bitch who's running the show, and it sure as hell isn't him. By this time tomorrow, he'll wish he had kept his ass in Savannah."

Chapter 20

We finally made it to our rooms, checked out each other's, and giggled like kids.

"Oh, Mitch, look at this wonderful balcony!"

"Mine's right next door, so we can open the partition and make it one huge outdoor space."

Mom's eyes sparkled. She was in her element, and I was sure this wouldn't be her one and only cruise.

"So, now what?"

I chuckled. "Why don't we unpack so our clothes aren't wrinkled beyond hope and then check out the ship as we set sail?"

"Yes, let's do that. Twenty minutes?"

"Sure, twenty minutes. I'll knock, and we'll go."

Once alone in my room, I made the call to Royce's office, and he answered right away.

"It's about time."

"What does that mean?"

"I've been waiting to hear what you learned from Mateo other than for us to buy the phones and have Tech put a tracker on his."

"I texted you last night that he was going to be in Tulum today and Puerto Morelos tomorrow. I said to find a drop location there and overnight the phones and money. I reminded you of the ship's name and my stateroom number in case the cell service was sketchy."

"Mitch, I never got that text. Are you sure it was sent?"

"Hang on. Let me check." I hit the text icon and saw that my last text to Royce was about Mateo being in Chetumal and that he was heading north on Friday. "Shit, it mustn't have gone through. Anyway, what I had said was that Mateo was heading to Tulum today, and tomorrow, he and his drug buddies will be in Puerto Morelos. The Federales need to be told that he fled the US since he's a drug smuggler who's murdered three people."

"How close is that town to where your ship is docking?"

"We pass it on our way to Playa del Carmen. I believe it's a half-hour car ride between the two cities."

"I'm sure the Federales in Puerto Morelos can pick him up. I'll find out, and keep your phone handy and check it often."

"Will do." I hung up, glanced at the screen on the burner phone for an unread text, saw none, and then met up with my mom. We set out to investigate every fun thing there was to do on our all-day-and-night cruise to Playa del Carmen.

Hours passed. We played shuffleboard, ping-pong, and bingo, walked the length of the ship on both sides, and relaxed by the pool. Between those activities, we enjoyed lunch and a couple of cocktails with umbrellas in them.

At four thirty, the burner phone buzzed against my leg. I

apologized to my mom and read the text. All it said was that Mateo had arrived in Tulum. I pocketed the phone within seconds.

"See, that wasn't so bad, was it? And reading it didn't put me in any danger."

"I know. Maybe I'm too protective, but you are my only son."

"And a cop, too, Mom. Don't forget that."

"Of course you are, and a damn good one I might add." She flagged down a roaming bartender and asked for two more umbrella drinks as we soaked up the sun.

I fired off a quick text to Royce saying that Mateo was in Tulum. I made sure it went through then placed the phone in my left pocket.

The rest of the day consisted of fun in the sun—or under a wide-brimmed hat in Mom's case. From our adjoining balconies, we planned to watch the sun dip beneath the horizon before we went down for supper.

It was five thirty when the last sliver of sun hit the water.

"Want to clean up for supper? Looks like the main dining room starts serving at seven o'clock. Tomorrow, we'll arrive in Playa del Carmen around ten in the morning."

"And I'm so excited to go on the Mayan ruins tour," Mom said.

I shook my head in awe as I thought about how most of those ruins were around a thousand years old. I could only imagine building those temples and cities with nothing but hand tools. It amazed me. "Yeah, that'll be pretty exciting. Marie has us scheduled to do the private tour that's more detailed instead of the big bus tour. It'll just be you and me on that one, and then the next day, we'll be doing that three-hour archaeological tour in Cozumel."

"That sounds great." Mom turned toward me and lifted her sunglasses. "Thanks for going out of your way, Mitch. I know you had reservations about coming, but I think we're doing just fine. Funny how we even like some of the same activities."

I wasn't about to say I would rather be snorkeling off a reef or zip-lining over a jungle canopy somewhere, but we were stuck on the ship anyway, so what was the harm? I made the best of the activities my mom wanted to do, and it was fun.

"Okay, I'm going to shower and change. Let's head downstairs at six thirty in case there's a long line."

She stood, motioned for me to stand, too, and gave me a tight squeeze. "I love you, Mitch Cannon."

I laughed. "And I love you, too, Mom."

Chapter 21

Mateo sat in one of the three rooms of the small dirt-floored house. They were on the northern outskirts of Tulum and would remain there that night. He needed time to think— and a plan. The original idea was to continue to Puerto Morelos tomorrow and stay there for the foreseeable future, but now that Mitch Cannon had thrown a wrench into the mix, Mateo needed to know more before moving on. Going to Puerto Morelos and possibly having Cannon, the FBI, or the Federales searching for him was too risky.

He inhaled his hand-rolled cigarette and blew rings of smoke while he waited for news. With his shoe, he squashed the bug that had just scurried across the floor.

Through the doorway, he watched as the old woman outside stirred a pot of beans over an open fire. She called out to the younger woman to prepare plates for Mateo and his two amigos, who sat on a bench nearby. Mateo rose and joined them before they completely lost the daylight. They thanked the women for the tortillas and beans then dug in.

After they had finished eating, Mateo's phone rang. Elan, the one Mateo had tasked with finding out more about

Mitch Cannon and his cruise itinerary, was calling.

"What do you have?" Mateo was short, curt, and to the point.

"I worked my connections. Tomorrow, they're taking a tour of the Tulum ruins." Elan laughed into the phone. "Just him and his mama on a private tour."

"That's perfect. What time do they meet the tour guide?"

"At one o'clock, and they're scheduled to return just before dark. The next day is a guided tour around Cozumel."

"Okay, and I know exactly what we'll do. Tomorrow morning, we'll gather here, I'll reveal my plan, and we'll move forward. I guarantee that Mitch Cannon will regret the day he ever crossed my path. He'll be squashed just like a bug under my shoe, and nobody will ever hear from him again." With a sadistic laugh, Mateo opened the cooler near his feet, pulled out bottles of beer, and passed them around. "Tomorrow at this time, Mitch Cannon and his mother will be nothing but distant memories. Drink up and get some rest. I want everyone on their game when we make our move."

Chapter 22

After supper, Mom and I said good night and retreated to our rooms. Although our day together had gone well, she and I were accustomed to our own space and our own time. It would be good to spend a few hours alone. I tipped my wrist and checked the time. The last text that had come in from Royce said they'd located a drop spot in Puerto Morelos on the corner of Condor and La Brea Streets. The store, El Rancho, was a send-and-receive location that also sold stamps, rented mailboxes, and offered fresh fruits and vegetables in their grocery section. Even though I would be contacting Royce after work hours and at home, it was necessary. I tapped his number.

"Hey, Boss," I said after he answered. "I got your last text a few hours ago. Was Tech able to put a tracking app on Mateo's phone, and is it and the money on their way?"

"They are, but since the Federales are going to snatch him up right at the store, were the phone and money even necessary?"

"Maybe and maybe not. He could show, he could send someone else to do the pickup, or the Federales might not get there on time. It's a good second measure in case of screwups. At least we'll be able to follow him and either get the FBI involved or make sure the Federales are doing their jobs and not on the take."

Royce groaned into the phone. "Honestly, I think the FBI is a better option. They can get there dressed as locals and swoop in. They'd have Mateo back in the good old US of A and in lockup by this time tomorrow night."

"True, but then we'd be off the case."

Royce huffed. "I'm over the one-upmanship shit. I don't care who takes him into custody as long as he's in cuffs and on an airplane back to American soil."

"I hear that. So, I'll text him the store name and location. Do you know what time the package is supposed to arrive at El Rancho?"

"By two o'clock tomorrow. It's already en route, and the Federales have been notified."

"Good. It sounds like everything is under control. I have a Mayan ruins tour to go on tomorrow with my mom, though."

"Doesn't matter, Cannon. The Federales said they'd rather you not help in the apprehension. Other people might be watching, which could put you in danger."

"As an American, you mean?"

"Exactly. You've been doing fine as the go-between. At this point, everything is set to move forward."

I sighed in relief. "Good, then I'll send off a text to Mateo where the location is and what time to be there. Talk to you soon."

"Thanks, Cannon, and good night."

I hung up and grabbed the burner phone off the nightstand. I tapped the words out in English, then after making sure it read exactly the way I wanted it to, I had the translation app switch it to Spanish. I hit Send, turned on the TV, and found a news station. At home, I normally drank a beer while watching the news. Marie was more of a wine drinker, but after the kids were in bed, she usually joined me in the living room to watch TV. I picked up the cabin phone and ordered two bottles of beer to be delivered to my room then pulled a five from my wallet as a tip. In a few minutes, other than the light movement I felt from the ship, it was as good as being at home, except I missed my pup. I was used to a snoring Gus balled up at the end of the couch.

Minutes later, I heard the sliding door to the balcony open from my mom's cabin. I paused the news, turned on the outdoor light, and saw her standing against the railing. My conversation with Rue popped into my mind. I'd promised not to let my mom stand against any railing unless I was at her side.

I opened my slider. "Mom?"

"Oh, honey, I didn't mean to disturb you, but can you turn off the light? I came out here to see the stars and moon without one single light interrupting their beauty."

"That's the best idea I've heard in I don't know how long. Care if I join you?"

She looked back at me. "I'd like nothing more."

"I have two beers coming from room service. I guess that's a sign, right?"

She chuckled. "You bet it is. Beer under the moonlight and listening to the ship push through the water. It's pure magic."

A knock sounded at my door. "There's more magic coming. I'll grab the beer and two glasses."

We reconnected that night, only for an hour, but it was a good hour. Mom reminisced about our childhoods and how Dad was such a force to deal with. She missed him, and I could hear it in her words.

"You're thirty-eight now, Mitch. Are you ever going to give me grandkids?"

I nearly choked on my beer. "I'll need to find a woman who wants to date me, marry me, and get pregnant first. It might be a while, Mom. You know how my last dating attempt went."

She shook her head. "What a nightmare."

I huffed. "That, it was, but at the time, with Marie and Devon missing, it was pretty scary."

"Do you think you'd ever give up being a cop, honey?"

"Nope. It's in my blood, and it's all I know to do."

"It sure gets dangerous at times, though." Mom took a swallow of beer and stared out to sea. "Looking out here right now at this beautiful ocean with the stars twinkling and the moon rays bouncing off the waves, it's hard to believe that evil can be found lurking around every corner."

I looked out and saw nothing but serenity. The water and sky blended as one, and the horizon had long disappeared. I had to admit it was beautiful, and I could have sat there all night and taken it in, but it was late, and we would be raring to go once the ship got to Playa del Carmen. We'd have a busy day tomorrow, and getting some sleep was probably the smart thing to do. I took both bottles and the glasses inside, said good night to Mom, and retreated to my room. Before I closed the slider, I asked her to promise me she wouldn't go out anymore that night.

"I don't want you to go out on the balcony alone, Mom."

"I won't. I promise. See you in the morning." She smiled, went inside, and closed her slider too.

Chapter 23

Over huevos rancheros, the men hatched the plan for the day. They knew they wouldn't have to look hard once the time came for the private tour. Other than the group tours in buses, it was likely that somebody would be standing alongside a van or SUV with a sign for Mitch Cannon in hand. Mateo would have several of his amigos watching the dock where the smaller boats brought the tourists in from the ship. The excursion vehicles had to wait just beyond the hotels. It would be a no-brainer, and Mitch Cannon and his mother wouldn't be the wiser.

Once the two were secured in the vehicle and on their way, they would be taken somewhere else, a remote location Mateo would choose, and even if they escaped, they would never find their way back to civilization.

Mateo and his men planned to head to the port a few hours early to see if the ship was in the harbor and if passengers were being ferried to the mainland for the day. Mitch Cannon and his mother might be checking out the shops beyond the beach before they left on their excursion. If they were spotted, it could be easier to snatch them without involving a tour guide, meaning one fewer person who could describe the kidnappers to the police.

Mateo confirmed his plan with the others. "We're leaving here at ten o'clock. It'll take almost an hour to reach Playa del Carmen, and that'll give us nearly two hours to see if Cannon has already left the ship. If I spot him, I'll call, and the plan to get him in our vehicles will go forward. If I don't spot him or if any of you don't see an American man with a woman who could be his mother, we'll continue with Plan B—find their tour guide, take him out, and wait for Cannon to come to us. Any questions?"

The men shrugged and looked at each other.

"I'll take that as a no." Mateo pointed his chin at the food. "Finish your breakfast, and we'll head out soon."

Chapter 24

I knocked on Mom's door at eight o'clock and smiled when she opened it. She was up and dressed in colorful clothes.

"Good morning, son. We're almost to Playa del Carmen!"

I laughed. "Yes, we are. By the time we finish breakfast and walk around for a bit, we'll be there. The ship will anchor out of the harbor, then the boats will ferry passengers to the dock. My question is, do you want to do some shopping and browsing before we go on our tour or stay on the ship until it's time to go?"

"Shop, of course! Let's go have breakfast. The sooner we're done eating, the sooner we can head out."

"Sounds like a plan."

We made our way to the dining room, where fifty people were already lined up and waiting to get in.

"Oh dear." Mom looked disappointed.

"It'll go fast, Mom. They're just trying to place people in groups without wasting empty seats." I laughed. "We're still out at sea, you know. There isn't much we can do until the ship reaches Playa del Carmen."

"I know. I'm just excited to get there."

Only fifteen minutes later, we were seated at a table for

six. We had three breakfast choices, or we could line up at the all-you-can-eat buffet station, which was already packed. Mom rolled her eyes.

"How about we pick from the menu? I wouldn't have gone back for seconds anyway."

"Good decision. I'm all for that."

We enjoyed our breakfast and conversation with our tablemates. We learned that two were teachers, two were a retired couple celebrating their fortieth wedding anniversary, and then there was Mom and me. I made sure to tell everyone that we were celebrating her seventieth birthday and that it was our first cruise. I'd mentioned that we were going on the Mayan ruins tour, and the others were too. Since we'd gotten to know them a little, I wished we were taking the bus tour, but Marie and Meg had booked the private tour, thinking it would be easier on Mom. We were sure to run into everyone during the tour anyway.

After breakfast, we said goodbye to the others and that we'd see them later at the ruins. Mom and I were going to walk around and watch the shoreline as we got closer.

"Are you enjoying the cruise, Mom?"

"Am I ever. This is the best birthday present I've ever had. I doubt that anything could top this."

"Glad to hear it. I'm having a great time too. So what do you have in mind for shopping?"

"Trinkets, gifts for the kids, that sort of thing."

The sun was bright, and a light salty breeze cooled us as we strolled the promenade deck. I pointed. "Check it out. I see land getting closer."

"We're there?"

"We will be soon. Let's grab some ship binos and take a look." We found a steward who gave us two sets to use, and we watched as the ship approached the harbor. We'd arrived, but it would take at least a half hour before they would be ready to transport passengers to land.

"We should get in line, Mitch, or we'll be waiting forever."

"Got everything you need for the day?"

"Shoot. I need my hat and sunglasses."

"Okay, let's get in line. You stay there and hold our spots, and give me your keycard. I'll grab your stuff and be back in a few."

Minutes later, after a mad dash to Mom's room and making sure I had both phones, I returned and located her in line just as the ship dropped anchor. She was the seventh person from the front, and as far back as I could see, people waited to disembark. Mom's suggestion to get in line early had been a good one. As we waited, I called Marie and updated her on the trip. I'd mentioned that we were going to shop at the stores along the harbor then go on the Mayan ruins tour at one o'clock. It promised to be a fun-filled day and one that we wouldn't soon forget. I promised to send pictures later. Mom pulled the phone from my hand so she could have a word with Marie.

"Hi, sweetheart. Guess what I'm wearing today? Yep, that new yellow top and those fun floral shorts. The weather is beautiful, the sky is clear, and it's about seventy-five degrees. We've got a light breeze too. Yes, Mitch went back to my cabin and grabbed my hat and sunglasses, and I have sunscreen wipes in my purse. I think we're in good shape."

I motioned for her to hang up. We had to show our IDs, sign out, and get off the ship. She said to give kisses to the kids then hung up and passed my phone back to me.

By eleven o'clock, we had our feet planted on Mexican soil. It felt good to have solid ground beneath us, and just beyond the large hotels were the gift shops. We headed out to enjoy a good hour and a half of shopping. After that, we would follow the signs to the bus parking area and watch for the driver who would take us on our Mayan ruins tour.

As we walked, I observed that every shop was nearly the same as the one before, but Mom didn't seem to notice. She was in her element. The streets were busy, and the pedestrian walkways were even busier since the passengers had left the ship. Mom picked out small Mexican dolls for Chloe and Lilly, a Mayan temple puzzle for Bryce, and for Della, a pink T-shirt that showed palm trees and the beach and had the words Playa del Carmen written across it.

"What do you think Marie and Meg would like, Mitch?"

I shrugged. "Something easy to pack, I'd say. T-shirts or tank tops, maybe? Or you can get them refrigerator magnets from the ruins."

"Ooh, that would be good and small enough to pack. I'll wait."

We continued on, stopped for ice cream, then shopped some more. We had about fifteen minutes before we needed to head to the parking lot. Mom was looking around.

"How far is the drive to the ruins?" she asked.

"About an hour and a half from here. Why?"

"I think I better find a restroom before we go."

"Sure. Let's head in that direction, and we should come across one."

We'd walked for another few minutes when I saw a sign that read Restrooms. "There they are, Mom, right where that sign is. I'll go, too, and meet you back out here in a few minutes."

She headed there since the line for the ladies' room was already growing. I tried on ball caps to help shield me from the sun. I found one, purchased it, then used the men's room. I waited outside the ladies' room for Mom to come out. After a few minutes, I checked the time.

Damn it, the driver has to be waiting for us.

I scanned the sea of shoppers for someone dressed like Mom—in a bright-yellow top and floral shorts. I tried to remember whether she was wearing her hat or carrying it, but either way, I didn't see her.

Chapter 25

Ten minutes earlier, Mateo's phone had rung. It was Elan saying he thought he'd spotted Cannon.

"I'll be right there and tell you if that's him." Mateo put on a large hat and headed to the shop along the walkway. A minute later, after watching across the aisles of the outdoor store, Mateo stared at the man trying on ball caps. "Yes, that's Cannon, but where's the mother?"

Elan pointed at the bathrooms. "She just walked out and headed left. I think she's under the impression that Cannon is in the men's room."

"Good. You have the sign?"

Elan nodded. "Cruz has it, and he's a half block away."

"Tell him to come in this direction and confront the woman in the yellow top and flowered shorts who's wearing a tan hat and sunglasses. He'll show her the sign and say that Mitch is waiting for her at the car."

"Yes, sir."

They stood back and watched as the interaction played out. Cruz held out the sign that read, "Mayan ruins tour for M. Cannon." The mother happily walked away with Cruz just as Cannon paid for the ball cap and went to the ladies' room to wait for her.

Mateo laughed. "This couldn't have played out better. Let's head that way. We need to be ready when Cannon shows up. He won't have a choice but to get into the car. Either he goes with you and Cruz, or you'll drive away with his precious mother, who he'll never see again."

Elan cocked his head as he watched Cruz and the mother head toward the parking lot. "My guess is that he'll be a willing passenger. You don't want us to let on who we are until we're away from civilization, right?"

"That's right, and we'll follow you and Cruz in the second car."

"Easy enough."

Chapter 26

I pulled aside a woman who had just left the ladies' room and described my mom to her. She said she hadn't noticed anyone fitting that description. My nerves were kicking in, and my stomach balled up. I didn't know if I should stay put or head to the parking lot. The crowd was thick, and it was hard to see beyond thirty feet, but Mom might have gone there to look for me.

I grabbed a napkin from a dispenser at a streetside bar and wiped the sweat from my forehead then slipped on my ball cap to block the sun and headed that way. The parking lot wasn't far, and if I didn't find her or the driver, I would retrace my steps to the restrooms.

As I got closer, relief washed over me. I saw a flash of a bright-yellow top and floral shorts climbing into an SUV.

"Thank God." I increased my pace and saw the man holding the sign. He nodded at me as I approached, and I smiled. "I thought for a second I lost my mom."

The back seat window went down, and Mom poked out her head. "I'm fine, honey. I kind of got lost, but this nice man found me. I thought you were already here at the car."

"Well, we're set now. Ready for the best day of your life?"

"I sure am, so get inside."

A minute later, a second man climbed into the SUV. After he took his spot in the passenger seat, the driver turned over the engine and pulled out of the parking lot.

"This is a two-man guided tour?" I was surprised.

"No, sir. I'm being dropped off at our headquarters down the road in a half hour."

"Oh, okay, thanks. How long is the tour?"

"Several hours, Mr. Cannon."

"Good. I'm looking forward to it."

The driver spoke up. "And so are we."

That was an odd response, but I assumed that anytime private tour groups got bookings, it was a good day. The driver headed south, just like I remembered seeing on the map, and our hour-and-a-half drive began. I wondered if either man would make conversation, tell us the history of the area, or remain quiet. So far, they hadn't said a word. Mom looked through the gifts she'd bought one more time, clearly happy with her purchases for the kids.

I gazed out over the ocean as we drove toward Tulum. Not a cloud in the sky, the ocean waves rolled lightly, and the bright sun caused the water to sparkle like it had been sprinkled with glitter. Small anchored boats bobbed up and down, and the yachts in the harbor made me wonder what life was like for the people who owned such impressive vessels. Farther in the distance, our cruise ship was still ferrying passengers. I sat back and realized that taking the trip with my mom was, and would be, a great experience. We would have stories to share when we got home and memories to embrace whenever the ocean called out to us. It was a good thing, and I felt like a jerk for having caused a stink about it. I hadn't realized how much I needed a vacation until we boarded the ship, and since then, my mind had actually relaxed. Catching Mateo Garcia was important, and I wouldn't forget that, and I hoped everything would go according to plan that day.

With a tip of my wrist, I checked the time. In a few short hours, the hunt for the criminal would be over, and Mateo would be in the custody of the Federales. I sighed. At least I hoped the plan would go forward without a hitch.

I glanced at my mom, and her head was back, and she was already dozing. I smiled and realized my own eyelids were growing heavy. I closed my eyes and, through the window, felt the sun warming the side of my face.

The bump we hit jarred me awake. I looked out and was surprised to see that the ocean wasn't to my left anymore. We were in a densely jungled area on a one-lane road. Both men were still in the front of the SUV.

I sat up straight. "Excuse me. Aren't we off course? The ruins are on the ocean."

The passenger looked over his left shoulder. "I need to be dropped off."

"Your headquarters are in the jungle? Wouldn't your business be hard to notice that way?"

The men remained quiet.

Mom stirred then woke up. She looked around. "Are we there?"

"No, Mom. Just hang tight while I talk to these guys." I checked the time again. An hour had already passed, yet I remembered the passenger saying that the headquarters, where he was being dropped off, were only a half hour from Playa del Carmen. I grabbed the back of the front seats and pulled myself within inches of the passenger's face. In front of us was nothing but thick, dark jungle. "Guys, what's up? This doesn't seem right."

The sudden upward thrust from the passenger's elbow to my chin threw me back against the seat. Mom screamed, and I tasted blood. I'd bitten my tongue. The SUV lurched to a stop, and both men climbed out.

My gut told me that we were being kidnapped, but how those strangers knew our names and that we had a land excursion booked that day was more than I could process. As they walked to the back of the vehicle, I followed them with my eyes. That was when I saw him. In that second, I knew the day would be far from the best one of my mom's life.

Mateo came to my side of the vehicle and pulled open the door. He gave me his best sinister grin and ordered us out. Mom was crying hysterically.

"Shut her up, or I will, Detective Cannon."

I couldn't wrap my mind around what was happening. Nothing was going according to plan. Mateo was supposed to be in Puerto Morelos, and we were supposed to be enjoying a Mayan ruins tour. Instead, our lives were in the hands of a murdering maniac and his amigos.

"Mom, Mom, please." I held my finger to my lips. "Don't say a word. Just take in a deep breath and remain quiet."

Mateo stuck out his hand. "Cell phones. Both of them and the old woman's too."

With shaking hands, I dug the phones out of my pockets and gave them to him. I couldn't understand how he knew I had two of them.

He jerked his chin toward my mom. "I won't ask her again."

Mom pointed at the SUV and, through tears, explained where her phone was. "It's in my purse in the vehicle."

Mateo nodded to one of his men, who then grabbed Mom's purse, rifled through it and removed her money then tossed the purse with the phone and wallet into the bushes.

"Give me your wallet, too, Cannon."

I did as he asked and remained silent. I knew what Mateo was capable of and didn't want to antagonize him. I watched as he pocketed my wallet then scrolled through the burner phone. He apparently recognized it as a match to his own—he knew it belonged to Luis. When he found what he was looking for, he laughed. "I bet your brain is about to explode. Right, Cannon? You're wondering how I figured out you were here and exactly where you'd be. You were so sure I'd be in Puerto Morelos today, right, *cerdo*?" His men laughed. "That means pig in Spanish in case you didn't know."

I remained quiet. Mateo was right—my brain was about to explode.

"Let me show you just how stupid you are. See, it isn't easy to keep two phones and play two identities, especially if you don't speak our language. Do you speak Spanish, Cannon?"

"No."

"Exactly. So you used a word translator?"

"Yes."

He chuckled and turned the phone toward me. "Read this out loud so your mama knows just how stupid you really are."

What I saw was the text I'd thought I sent to Royce, but I had actually written and sent it using the wrong phone. That was why Royce never got it.

"Read it!" Mateo yelled, his spit sprinkling my face.

My voice cracked as I began. "Boss, Mateo will be in Tulum on Friday and Puerto Morelos on Saturday, where he plans to hunker down. He said the town is small, off everyone's radar, and he has drug connections there. Let the Federales know he's a drug smuggler who killed three people in Savannah then fled south. In case you forgot or if the cell service is sketchy, I'm on the *Evening Star Princess*, in stateroom 319, and it'll reach Playa del Carmen tomorrow morning."

Mateo stared at my mom. "What's your name, old woman?"

"Mary."

"Well, Mary, aren't you proud of your son? Without that text he sent to me by mistake, you wouldn't be in this position. You'd be enjoying the afternoon in Tulum, and I'd probably be in handcuffs before the day is over. What do you have to say to that loser?"

She turned to me with tears in her eyes. "I love you, honey."

Chapter 27

It was clear that Mateo was calling the shots. The men with him obeyed like he was a kingpin, and maybe there was more to Mateo Garcia's life south of the border than we Americans realized.

"Turn around and put your hands behind your backs."

I did as Mateo ordered.

"You, too, Mary, or I'll have my men manhandle you." He laughed at his way with words.

"Just do it, Mom," I whispered. "I'm so sorry—"

"Shut up! Nobody gave you permission to speak."

I winced as the man Mateo called Cruz, the driver to our hellhole, cinched the zip ties around my wrists. I knew Mom would cry out if he tightened hers as much as he did mine.

"Can you go easy on her?" I asked.

Immediately, I got a blow to the back of my head and dropped to my knees. Mom began crying again, and all I could do was shake my head in hopes that she would stop.

I watched as Cruz zip-tied her hands behind her back. I was sure she was in pain, but she kept it to herself.

"Get up," Mateo ordered. He grabbed a backpack out of

his vehicle and tossed it to Cruz.

I stood, somewhat wobbly but with both feet under me. He ordered us into the "tropical forest," as the guidebooks called them, but to me, they were dense jungles that I was sure were full of venomous spiders, snakes, lizards, and bugs. That alone would give Mom a heart attack if the fear of those men and the trek through the tangled brush didn't. I was sure they weren't carrying machetes just for blazing trails.

I noticed a holstered gun on Mateo's hip. The man who rode in the car with him also carried a gun. I hadn't caught his name yet. The two from our car, Cruz and Elan, weren't carrying firearms, at least not that I could tell, but the machetes they held were threatening enough. I wondered where we were going that the vehicles could be left behind like that. Before they pushed us on, I looked back and saw that the road ended just beyond the cars. Then I realized it wasn't a road we were on at all—just a long driveway of sorts hidden within the jungle.

It was hopeless. We didn't have phones, weapons, or anything whatsoever to defend ourselves with. Our hands were tied behind our backs, making us completely vulnerable to whatever happened, whether intentional or not.

Cruz and Elan took the lead, using the machetes to whack through the thick brush, although there looked to be a trail in front of them already. I wondered if they'd been back there earlier and our destination wasn't far into the jungle or if it was nothing more than an animal path.

I listened and noticed that my hearing had become much more keen. The jungle sounds, bird calls, and rustling noises just beyond my sight all caught my attention. I worried about my mom—she feared animals except for domestic ones like cats and dogs—and we were in an unfriendly environment with who knew what kind of insect, animal, reptile, or human that could do us harm.

We walked for about fifteen minutes and went deeper into the jungle. I couldn't say how far we'd gone since most of the trek involved climbing over downed limbs or tripping on vines. I didn't know if it was best to have Mom behind me so I could clear the way or ahead of me so I could keep my eye on her. If we got out of our predicament alive, I wondered whether our efforts to get closer and spend more time together would be over. Would Mom hate me and never speak to me again as I'd feared Marie would do when she was kidnapped, or would she forgive me after the job I loved had put my family in danger? There was a chance that I would never know.

As we walked, I racked my brain about how Royce might be alerted to our predicament. By then, the Federales must have told him that Mateo was a no-show at the bodega in Puerto Morelos. Royce would be trying to reach me and wouldn't be able to. That would be warning enough that something was wrong unless he'd think the trip to the ruins was out of cell phone range.

Maybe he sent a text, continued with whatever he was doing, and didn't check for a response yet, but since I don't have a phone anymore, there's no way to know anything.

A million questions and scenarios were running through my mind, and there wasn't a damn thing I could do about a single one. I rubbed my cheek against my shoulder. The mosquitos were plentiful and buzzed in and out of my ears and all around my face. They were bad, but from what I'd read in the tour guides, they were worse during the rainy season—April through November. I thanked God it wasn't raining since Mom would surely lose it in those conditions.

Minutes later, Cruz and Elan slowed to a stop ahead of us. Elan turned back and yelled over his shoulder. I tried to see past him, but the trail had thinned, and the jungle had become even thicker. After pushing us aside, Mateo went to the front, where he spoke to the men in Spanish. I had no idea what the conversation was about, but it seemed there was a chance that something was blocking the path or we had gone as far as we were going. I couldn't see my wrist to know how much time had passed, but I guessed we had walked for twenty minutes or so.

Mateo turned back and grinned. "We're here, and now it's time for you two to get comfortable in your new home." He nodded to the man at our backs, who pushed us forward.

Ahead, a weathered canvas tarp was tied to the tree canopy about seven feet high, and several dirty old buckets lay on a rotting wooden platform.

"Back in the day, this was where we manufactured our cocaine. Of course, it was well-equipped and had many more stations then." Mateo looked around. "Between the Federales and nature, there isn't much left, but it'll be fine for you." He looked at my mom. "And her. Do you like your new home, Mary?"

Mom remained silent.

"Answer me, you old hag!"

I tipped my head at her. With tears running down her sweat-covered face, Mom said she liked it.

"Good. Glad to oblige." Mateo jerked his chin toward Cruz. "Secure them. Give each of them a bottle of water, set a bucket next to them, and then text Alejandro. I want to know every detail of what happened in Puerto Morelos. Tell him to text you back and then meet us at the house by the cenotes in two hours."

With guns pointed at our heads in case we tried to escape, the original zip ties were removed, and each of us had a new one secured to one wrist with a chain entwined through it, wrapped around the base of a tree, and padlocked. That allowed us a small amount of mobility to use the buckets as toilets and to open our water bottles. We were about ten feet apart, with just enough chain to make it to the wooden platform but no chance of reaching each other. I had no way to comfort my mom through the night, which I was sure would be long, cold, and scary.

I yelled out as the men were walking away. "How about a flashlight? It's the least you can do."

Mateo laughed. "You give me way too much credit. Do I really look like I give a shit? Enjoy your night, Cannon."

Chapter 28

Royce stormed into Rue's office. "Nobody other than the Federales showed up at the drop location."

A look of concern swept across Devon's face. "There's no way Mateo could have known it was a setup. What do you think happened?"

Royce blew out an angry puff while pacing the small area between the door and the desks. "Hell if I know. Trying to understand the broken English of the head honcho was nearly impossible. I fired off a text to Cannon, asked if he could make a connection via a phone call to the local police in Puerto Morelos and ask if they could tell him more. I'm sure he won't have an easier time of understanding them than I did unless there's a fluent English-speaking person there."

"Get a response back from Mitch yet?"

Royce shook his head. "Damn it. It's all my fault for telling him not to show up there, but he's on vacation for God's sake. Nothing like ruining it for his mom, and they had already booked a tour of the Tulum ruins for today."

"Right. So now what?"

"Unless there's no phone reception in that area, I'd think

he'd either call or at least text back," Royce said.

"I don't think the Riviera Maya region is like a third world country. The area has a lot of tourism, and I'm sure they have cell reception. Maybe give him a half hour to respond. They might be in the middle of their guided presentation, plus I think Mitch is trying to be courteous to his mom."

"Yeah." Royce set his phone alarm for three o'clock. "There. I'll give him another forty-five minutes to text me back, then I'll try again."

"When did you talk to him last?"

"Early last night. I gave him the name and location of the drop spot. He said he'd text it to Mateo right away. That's really it, just a five-minute conversation."

"Humph... I'm sure if anything went wrong, Cannon would have texted you or me."

Royce scratched his cheek as he thought. "You're right. He's enjoying his vacation and rightfully so. He does deserve one every now and then." Royce patted the doorframe before walking out. "I'll let you know if I hear from him."

"And Luis still won't talk?"

"Nope. He's probably worried about retaliation if he did. I'm afraid he'll take the rap and accept his fate."

"He might get shivved in prison."

"True enough. I can't say it wouldn't do my heart good if he did." Royce returned to his office to wait.

Forty-five minutes passed, the timer went off, and still no text or call from Cannon. Royce looked from his phone to the wall clock and back at the phone. He didn't want to become irrational about the lack of communication, especially since Cannon had said the tour would take several hours and they were going to see the cenotes before returning to Playa del Carmen. They wouldn't return to the ship until just before dark.

Feeling antsy, Royce headed down to SVU. He needed to find the officer who was fluent in Spanish, call the Federales back, and have them explain everything that had happened in Puerto Morelos that day. The officer could repeat it back to Royce once he ended the phone call.

With the call in process, Royce took time to contact Bleu at home. "Chuck, I need a word of advice."

"Yeah, shoot."

"Turns out that the takedown in Puerto Morelos was an enormous failure. Mateo never showed."

"Son of a bitch. Was he tipped off?"

"It appears that way, but how and by whom, I don't know."

Bleu huffed into the phone. "That's a damn good question. You sure Cannon texted him the location and time?"

"I have no reason to think he didn't. He told me he was going to text him as soon as we got off the phone last night. Haven't spoken to him since."

"Call him."

"I've tried calling and texting. Either the message isn't going through, or he just hasn't had the opportunity to call or text back."

"That seems odd. Cannon is always on the ball, even if it's only a text."

Royce sighed and continued. "Anyway, I have Juan

Ramirez from SVU talking to the Federales. I couldn't understand half of what the commander was saying to me earlier."

"Maybe it was their fault. They could have come in like stormtroopers and scared Mateo away before they even put eyes on him."

"Maybe. We'll see what Ramirez has to say when the call is over with."

"Do you need anything from me right now?"

Royce jiggled the change in his pocket—a nervous habit. "Nah, I'll see you at five thirty. Thanks, buddy."

"No sweat."

Royce pocketed his phone and returned to the SVU office that Ramirez had called from. He found the officer still on the phone with Pedro Torres, the commander in charge of the takedown. As Royce leaned against the doorway and watched a fly buzz on the window, he waited.

Several minutes later, and with Timmons listening in, Ramirez explained what the commander had told him. He'd said that there were nine of them, six standing out of sight a block from the store. Three dressed in civilian clothes went inside and appeared to be shoppers. The store owner was aware of what was about to take place, and the federal police assured him that he wouldn't be in danger. Whether he'd tipped off Mateo, because his connections were far and wide, or Mateo's own men had arrived early and were also watching from a distance, they would likely never know. They stayed in the area until three thirty with no sightings of Mateo Garcia and nobody stepping up to the counter to claim the shipment.

"So, no matter what, he didn't show up and take the bait even with five hundred bucks included in the package?"

"Apparently not, Sergeant Royce. Commander Torres said they would watch the store for one more day, and if Garcia didn't show or if one of his amigos didn't come in to claim the package, he'd send it back to you unopened."

"Okay. Thanks for making the call."

Royce trudged up the stairs with a worried mind. He returned to his office, tried Mitch's phone once more with a simple text that read, *Did you get my message from earlier?* and hit Send.

He called Rue, told him the gist of the conversation, and felt his stomach roll. Worry was settling into his gut.

"Should I call Marie and find out if she's talked or texted with Mitch or her mom today?" Devon asked.

"Are you on close enough terms that she won't think calling her is odd?"

"Well, we're friends. I'll just ask if Mitch has sent pictures that she could forward to me. All the jealous cops want to see what somebody looks like who's been given vacation time."

Royce chuckled. "Yeah, yeah, not a bad idea, but you make me sound like a real hardass. Go ahead. Do it and get right back to me." Royce hung up, and Devon took the reins.

Rue checked the time—nearly four o'clock. He scrolled through his cell phone contacts until he found Marie's name. He'd left off the last name when he'd programmed it into his phone since she'd mentioned going back to Marie Cannon after her divorce was final. With a tap on her name, the phone rang on her end.

"Hello?"

"Marie, it's Devon."

"Hey, Devon. What's up?"

Rue wanted to sound lighthearted even though he was actually on a fishing expedition. "Just wondering when you spoke to Mitch or your mom last."

"Is something wrong?" Her voice took on a higher pitch.

"No, not at all. Just asking."

"Um, this morning, I guess. Yeah, it was this morning. They were in line to get on the ferry boats to the mainland. They'd just gotten to Playa del Carmen. I'm so jealous now that I didn't go."

Devon laughed. "I hear that. I bet Mitch will gain ten pounds on that all-inclusive 'eat whenever you want and drink all day' kind of cruise. So that was this morning, huh?"

"Yep."

"Have they sent you any pictures yet that you care to share? The guys here want to see what a real cop on vacation looks like."

Marie laughed into the phone. "Actually, Mitch promised to send some from the ruins, but I haven't gotten any yet, that turkey. How cool would that be to see those ruins up close and personal, though. Right?"

"Absolutely. Well, when you get them, can you send some over?"

"Of course I will. I hope your guys don't get too jealous. I mean, he's with my mom, not a girlfriend."

"But sometimes, that removes the pressure to overdeliver or please."

Marie laughed again. "True enough. Anything else? I was just about to pop these cupcakes into the oven."

"Yum, and no. Looking forward to seeing those pics, though. Thanks, Marie."

"You bet."

Devon hung up and let Royce know that Marie had spoken to Mitch that morning shortly before they left for the tour. He'd promised pictures, and she was still waiting, which didn't make either of them feel any better.

Chapter 29

It was after six when Royce finally left the precinct. He caught up with Rue, and they discussed their uneasy feelings as they crossed the parking lot together.

"I told Bleu to call me if any news comes into the station. Keep your phone handy and on ring mode all night in case Cannon tries to contact you."

"I will, and this definitely isn't like Mitch. Even if our messages didn't get through to him, you would think he'd stay in touch anyway and keep us updated about his contact with Mateo."

Royce grunted as he kicked a rock across the pavement and watched it spin. "You would think."

They parted ways at their vehicles and drove off, each in a different direction.

Devon thought back to the time he and Marie had been held captive by the crazy brother-and-sister team of Marlon Reyes and Liza Montclaire. There was no way he could call for help because his phone had been taken away. There wasn't a way to free himself either—he was secured in a fifty-gallon barrel. Experience told him that silence was usually an indicator of something bad.

Could Mitch and Mary actually be in trouble with no way to let us know? Is that why there hasn't been any communication with either of them since early this morning? And what happened to the pictures Marie was going to forward to me? Did Mitch ever send them?

Deep in thought, Rue jumped when his phone rang. He grabbed it and checked the screen, hoping it was Mitch, but it wasn't. It could be good news or bad, and he would know as soon as he said hello.

"Marie, have you gotten those pictures yet?" Devon tried to sound positive.

Silence filled the line for several seconds. At that moment, he knew which way the conversation was about to go.

"Marie?"

Her voice cracked. "I guess Mitch listed me to the ship personnel as their contact person in the States. You know, for emergency reasons."

"Yeah, and?"

"And I just got a call that he and Mom never returned to the ship after their Mayan ruins tour. The ship liaison said they're fifty minutes overdue, yet all the bus tour riders have returned. It was the same tour, but I thought the private one would have been easier for Mom. Why the hell did I schedule it for them? The driver might have had a flat tire or hit something on the road. Who knows? I was told the ship will wait one more hour, and then they're going to leave for Cozumel. Wouldn't Mitch have called the ship if he knew they'd be late?"

"I'd think so. Do you have the contact information for the private tour driver and the company name?"

"Yes. Hold on while I get it." Marie left the phone for several minutes.

During that time, Devon pulled over and had his notepad and pen ready to go.

"Okay, I'm back. Are you ready?"

"Yep, go ahead."

Marie rattled off the names of the tour company and the driver. "Please call me when you find out something."

"I promise I will. Give me a half hour or so." Devon hung up and immediately dialed Royce. "Boss, we have a problem."

"Shit. Tell me what's wrong."

While he drove, Rue explained to Royce what Marie had just told him. "I'm about to call the tour driver and ask what's going on. Either he had car trouble, or he dropped off Mitch and Mary back at the dock and something happened before they boarded the ship."

"That doesn't explain the entire day of silence, though."

"You're right, Sarge. It sure doesn't."

"Call me back after you talk to him," Royce said.

"Will do."

Rue was less than five minutes from home. It would be easier to call, take notes, and ask questions while sitting at the table with a sturdy surface and a larger piece of paper in front of him.

Once home, he grabbed a beer, a sheet of copy paper, and the notepad on which he'd written down the information from Marie. His nerves had already hit overdrive.

From what he'd written down, the tour company was Castillo's Riviera Maya Private Tours, and that day's driver was Carlos Hernandez. He dialed the company first. Devon assumed that if the driver had car trouble, he would have called it in.

The woman who answered began her greeting in Spanish, and Rue asked if she spoke English. She said she did.

"How may I help you, sir?"

"My friend and his mother had a private tour for the Tulum ruins booked with Carlos Hernandez today. The ship's liaison just informed my friend's sister that they never returned to the ship. They're way overdue."

"May I have their names please?"

"Yes, Mitch and Mary Cannon."

"Please hold while I look up Carlos's schedule for today."

Rue took a swig of beer and tapped his pen against the table while he waited.

"Sir?"

"Yes, I'm here."

"It seems that your friends were a no-show for the tour, so Carlos booked something else with a family of four at two o'clock."

"What! You're absolutely sure?"

"Yes, sir. He's already clocked out and gone home for the day. According to our policy for no-shows, we can only refund fifty percent of the tour cost to the credit card it was booked with."

"Understood, and thank you." Rue hung up and squeezed his temples. Something bad had happened. Mitch and Mary were supposed to meet with the driver at one o'clock. Devon glanced at his watch and groaned.

That was six hours ago. I need to call Royce back right away.

He tapped his boss's cell number and waited for only a second before Royce picked up.

"So, what did the driver say?"

"I called the company instead. They said Mitch and Mary were no-shows for the tour. They never met at the driver's car after they left the ship."

"Shit, and the liaison who spoke with Marie was sure they actually disembarked?"

"Yes. Everyone who leaves the ship has to sign out and then sign back in when they return. They signed out but never signed back in."

"Maybe they forgot to."

"Nope. The purser sits at the ship entrance as the passengers reboard. They can't get past him until they sign in."

"And they checked their rooms?"

"Yep, and they aren't there. They even paged them to the passenger services area, and nobody showed up. They aren't on the ship, Boss, and they didn't go on the tour. Between the time they got off the ferry onto Mexican soil and the time they should have gone on the tour, they vanished into thin air."

"Son of a bitch. Have you called Marie back yet?"

Rue muttered a few curse words before saying no. "I guess that'll be next. If something bad happened to Mary and Mitch, Marie and Meg will never forgive themselves for arranging the cruise."

"I'm guessing it's a kidnapping, but I'm under the impression that the area around the hotels and stores is highly populated when the cruise ships come in," Royce said.

"Probably so, but if somebody holds you at gunpoint, what are you going to do?"

"Yell for help? Fight back? I'd imagine Mitch would."

"Unless they snatched Mary first and then made Mitch go along quietly. That might have been his only choice if he wanted to see his mother alive again."

Royce groaned into the phone. "I'll call the consular agency in Playa del Carmen and see what they can do. Meanwhile, as much as you won't want to make the call, you need to let Marie know what's happened."

Rue let out a heavy sigh. "Yes, sir, and I'll talk to you later."

Just as Devon was about to call Marie, he changed his mind, got in his car, and headed to Mitch's house. What had happened to Mitch and Mary was still an unknown, but unsettling news needed to be shared in person.

The kids would still be up, but he was sure Marie could coax them into watching a movie while they talked privately. It was Saturday night, and Della and Chloe didn't have school the next day. A good movie and some ice cream should convince them to stay in the living room while he told Marie what he'd learned. Devon pulled into Stop and Shop, grabbed a quart of chocolate chip mint ice cream, and headed out again. He would be at Mitch's house in under five minutes.

Chapter 30

Gravel crunched under his tires as Rue pulled into the driveway. His headlights bounced off the house, and he saw Marie move the kitchen curtain aside and look out. He was sure she wouldn't come to the door after dark, so he sent a quick text saying he was outside. Seconds later, Marie opened the slider and allowed him in.

"Not that I mind, but what the heck are you doing here, Devon?"

He tipped his head toward the kitchen. "We need to talk privately. I brought ice cream for the kids."

"Damn it. That means bad news is coming."

"Hold it together, Marie, and get the kids settled. I'll explain everything I know after that."

They entered the house together, then Della and Chloe stormed into the kitchen. They were excited to see Devon and gave him hugs, then Marie filled two bowls with ice cream, found a movie for them to watch, and said she and Devon needed to talk adult talk. The kids had to stay in the living room.

"Don't make a mess in there either and keep the volume

down." Marie turned toward Devon. "Let's go into the kitchen, and I'll pour us some coffee."

He waited until she'd sat down before he spoke.

"Okay, just rip the bandage off. What the hell happened, and don't beat around the bush."

He took a sip of coffee, sat the cup down, and began. "All we know is that after you spoke to Mitch and your mom this morning, they both vanished."

Tears pooled in Marie's eyes then slid down her cheeks. "What exactly does that mean?"

"They never took the tour to the ruins. According to the tour company, the driver waited for them, they never showed, so he took a family on a different tour. He never saw Mitch or your mom."

"You're sure? Maybe that driver kidnapped them!"

"It's documented with the driver and the company that they were a no-show. They left the ship and haven't been seen since."

"They were going to shop before the tour. It sounds like that area has tons of kiosks, stores, and restaurants. Two people among hundreds can't just up and disappear. Mitch is a cop for God's sake. Plus, he'd never let anything happen to our mom."

Rue stared into his cup.

Marie was becoming frantic. "What aren't you telling me?"

Rue gave a quick glance toward the living room, saw that the kids hadn't heard Marie, and put his finger to his mouth. "Keep it down. You don't want the kids to know anything is off until we actually know that ourselves. We're suspecting a kidnapping. Has anyone called you today that you don't know or maybe a blocked call that you didn't pick up?"

"No, at least not that I know of. I don't have my phone glued to my side twenty-four hours a day."

"Can you check for missed calls?"

"Yeah." Marie stepped to the kitchen counter, pulled the phone off the charger, and fumbled with it. Her fingers trembled. She shook her head and looked at Devon. "No missed calls."

"Okay, that might be a good sign."

"How in God's name can that be a good sign? They've vanished!"

Rue held up his hands, his palms facing her. He leaned in and whispered. "Because kidnappers normally take the person's phone, find a relative, and call with a ransom demand. That hasn't happened yet, and they've been missing for over six hours."

"That doesn't make me feel any better." Marie rose from the table, went to the cabinet, and pulled out two shot glasses. She opened the upper cabinet and poured from Mitch's whiskey bottle, spilling some in the process. "I'm so damn nervous I can't even pour this without spilling it."

"Keep calm. We have to think of this in a logical way."

Marie gulped the whiskey and slid Devon's glass across the table. He passed it back.

"I have to keep a clear head."

She gulped his.

"Okay, that's enough. You have two kids here you need

to take care of." Devon got up, put away the whiskey, and placed the shot glasses in the sink. "I'm thinking it might have been a random kidnapping because Mary was easy prey, but if they aren't demanding anything yet, then I'm not so sure."

Marie shook her head. "They might have called somebody else on Mitch's contact list or even on my mom's."

"I'd think we would have heard about it by now, though."

Marie topped off both coffee cups.

"Other than Mitch's work contacts, which a kidnapper wouldn't know were cops, do you think your contact lists are close to the same?"

"Probably, and Mom's too."

"Then I need to take a picture of your contacts."

Marie passed her phone to Devon, and he snapped off the names and numbers of her twenty-two person contact list.

"I should go. Royce was going to call the consular agency in Playa del Carmen. It's the closest one that may be able to help or at least find the right people for us to speak with."

"Does their disappearance have anything to do with Mateo Garcia?"

Rue looked surprised. "I didn't know Mitch shared that information with you."

"Only a little bit. That's why he didn't want to go on the cruise. It was because of the investigation regarding the murders Mateo committed."

Devon's mind was racing. He knew that somehow, someway, Mitch and Mary's disappearance was related to Mateo. It was the only thing that made sense. Somebody had tipped him off that Mitch was in Mexico, and that was why Mateo didn't show at the store to pick up the package.

Devon stood, thanked Marie for the coffee, and headed to the door.

"That's it? You're just leaving me with all this worry? What am I supposed to say to Meg?"

"Give me until tomorrow. I'm going to run some ideas past our team and see what we can find out. I'll call you before noon and give you an update. For now, stay safe, make sure all the doors are locked, and keep your phone at your side at all times."

"You're scaring me."

Devon gave Marie's hand a squeeze. "I'm not trying to, but I need to keep my mind on Mitch and your mom. You need to do your part to protect yourself and the kids."

She nodded. "You're right, and we'll be okay."

Devon said good night to Chloe and Della then walked out. He turned back before Marie closed the door. "I want to hear you turn that dead bolt." He waited, listened for the click, then continued to his car.

On the ten-minute drive home, he would call Royce. Rue wanted to hear what the consular agency had to offer and run past Royce his idea of Mateo being involved in Mitch's disappearance.

Royce answered right away and said he was just walking into his house. He'd spoken with the consular agency, which gave him the phone number of the Playa del Carmen police station and the commander in charge. The man Royce had spoken to was sure there were cameras along the pedestrian walkway where all the stores and restaurants were located because pickpockets ran rampant in that area, especially when the cruise ships came in.

"Have you called the police yet?" Rue asked.

"I will as soon as I get situated in the house. Have you spoken to Marie?"

Rue groaned. "Yeah, and I asked her to sit tight and not talk to Meg about this yet, especially since we don't even know what *this* is. She did bring something to light, though, that may hold merit."

"Really? And what's that?"

"That Mateo might have his hand in Mitch and Mary's disappearance."

"Mitch talks to her about his investigations?"

"I doubt if he goes into detail. This was an isolated case. He wasn't all that stoked about going on the cruise simply because of Mateo shooting Cynthia and her kids."

"Humph. Mateo knew to stay away from the pickup location in Puerto Morelos too. How he figured that out is still unknown. If Marie is right, then somebody tipped off Mateo that it was a setup and that Mitch was on that cruise ship."

Rue let out an irritated huff. "And figuring out how he knew that is the million-dollar question. Other than us at the PD, who knew about Luis's burner phone and that we had it in our possession? Nobody knew Mitch was going on that Mexican cruise except us and his family. There's somebody feeding Mateo information, but for the life of me, I can't think of who that could be."

Chapter 31

I listened to the jungle noises with deep concern. As darkness took over and the sounds heightened, I worried about my mom. I couldn't see her any longer, and if something did come by to investigate us, there was nothing I could do to help. We shared stories to soothe each other and get our minds off the danger lurking out of sight. The jungle was pitch-black, and beyond several feet, I couldn't see anything. I knew there were panthers in Mexico, particularly in the Yucatan Peninsula, and plenty of them, but I wasn't about to tell Mom. Sharing that information would send her into a frenzy and possibly attract curious animals.

The whispering I heard caused me to cock my ear in Mom's direction. She was praying for our safety, and my heart broke. As usual, it was because of me that my loved ones found themselves in danger. Why trouble followed me, I didn't know. I wasn't particularly abrasive to the killers we caught, no more than anyone else in our department, but killers were a breed all their own. They were a special kind of crazy that never forgot who arrested them, who interrogated them, and who testified against them in court. Maybe it was because I was the lead detective and came face-to-face with the bad guys more often, but I was only guessing.

Our predicament was entirely on me, though. Through my rush to spend time with my mom and not piss her off on her birthday cruise, I'd been reckless and inattentive. It was my fault that I sent the text meant for Royce through the burner phone instead of my own. It had gone directly to Mateo, and that was a deadly mistake. As a result, Mom sat in the jungle only feet from me with danger all around us, yet I couldn't keep her safe. Any kind of predatory animal could creep up on us. I prayed too—for daylight to come quickly.

Maybe it was time to retire and find another occupation, one free of risk. One where I didn't have to work ten or more hours a day and nearly every weekend. One where I didn't have to worry about the job affecting my family, and one that actually allowed me to spend time with them.

If we ever get out of this, that's something I'll have to give serious consideration to. Family is everything, I've always said. Maybe it's time to live up to my words.

"Mitch?"

"Yes, Mom."

"Do you ever pray, honey?"

"I do, but it seems that I only pray when someone is in trouble, and I know that's wrong. I should pray anyway and thank God for our health, our love of family, the beautiful city and world we live in, and the moon and stars we enjoyed last night from the balcony."

"That was only last night?"

"It was, but it seems like a lifetime ago, doesn't it?"

"Uh-huh. Mitch, are we going to live through this?"

I wiped my eyes and was glad she couldn't see the worry on my face. "Of course we are."

"Why does that man hate you so much?"

"He's a criminal, Mom, and criminals don't think straight."

"But you only deal with murderers."

"Right, but I knew him from a long time ago."

"Then why were you on a case now that involves him?"

Even though my mom was seventy, she was as smart as a whip, and there wasn't much that got past her.

"He killed somebody, didn't he?"

I couldn't lie my way through her questions, and I sighed before answering. "He's the man who shot and killed the mother and her two kids in Savannah last week. The man who kidnapped us is the man I was tracking, the one I told you about."

The woman who was as tough as nails throughout my entire life was beginning to crumble. She wept openly then prayed again. "I can't watch him kill you. If it comes to that, I'll demand he kill me first. You're my youngest child, my only son, and I can't bear to think of our fate. If I had a way, I'd kill myself now so he wouldn't have the pleasure of doing it."

"Mom, stop, please. We're going to get through this, I promise you."

"You can't make that promise. Only God can."

"Then keep praying, and pray that the jungle animals spare us too."

I sat awake most of the night. What seemed like forever

was likely only a few hours. My head bobbed several times, but I forced myself to stay awake for my mom's sake. When I heard her crying, I tried to get her to focus on something else—to tell stories of our youth, to share fun memories, and to tell me how Dad proposed. I needed to hear the stories I'd never asked about, and in hindsight, I was ashamed that I never had.

"What was life like back in the fifties, growing up with Grandpa and Grandma?"

Mom chuckled. "They were tough but hardworking people. They made us kids toe the line, that's for sure. No allowance, and we did chores because we were told to. We pulled our weight, helped out, and obeyed. Nothing like the kids these days who run the household and live off their folks until they're thirty. At least we did one thing right as parents."

"Yeah, what's that?"

"Dad and I raised you three to be responsible adults with good values and judgment. Marie and Meg are good mothers too. They don't let the kids smart off, and those children respect their elders. You three are honest, moral, and hardworking, just like my mom and dad raised us to be."

Mom couldn't see me smiling, but I was and told her so.

"I wish I had grown up in the fifties. Life was slower, people were friendlier, and crime wasn't as commonplace as it is now. I've never understood the saying about how a town is so safe people don't lock their doors at night. Small town or not, it only takes a minute to lock the doors to ensure your safety."

Mom laughed. "We always locked the doors at night.

Hell, we had precious cargo inside the house—our kids. Who wouldn't protect their children?"

I remembered what we had been told about the scene at Cynthia's house and how she'd tried to shield her teens from Mateo, yet they all died. If I had one dying wish, it would be that Mateo died alongside me and at my hand.

"Try to get some sleep, Mom, since we have no idea what tomorrow will bring. I'll stay awake and do what I can to keep us safe."

"When will those men come back, and what will they do?"

I shook my head even though she couldn't see me. If only I had the answers she was looking for. "I have no idea how to answer either question, but if there's a chance in hell, I'll get us out of this mess."

Chapter 32

"You up for going back to the station?" Royce asked.

"Yeah, why not? A half-dozen heads trying to come up with answers is better than us sitting alone and accomplishing nothing. I wouldn't be able to sleep tonight anyway."

"Good, then eat supper and head back. I'll be there by nine o'clock."

"You got it."

Forty-five minutes later, they gathered around the conference room table. Both sergeants were in attendance—Royce and Bleu. Devon, Bob Prentice, and Ricky Bloom were there too.

Royce updated the group on what he knew, which wasn't much except that Mitch and Mary had been missing since eleven o'clock that morning. The consular agency in Playa del Carmen gave him the phone number of the local police and name of the commander, Roberto DeLeon, whom Royce had asked for when he called. He was told that the commander worked the day shift hours and would have to give the orders for his police force to search the city for an American man and his mother who were there as tourists.

"How about the Federales? We've already had communication with Pedro Torres, the commander in charge of Mateo's takedown," Rue said.

"The takedown that was a bust? Our credibility with him probably diminished a lot after that."

"Doesn't matter. An American police detective and his mother have gone missing on Mexican soil. They have to put out a search for them."

"I'll call the FBI," Bleu said. "The more irons in the fire to find Mitch and Mary, the better. Time wasted will only make it tougher to track them down. The Yucatan has dense jungles and wild animals. They could be anywhere, and God help them if they're out in that dangerous environment alone at night."

Royce agreed. "The Federales have to know who the worst criminals are in that area. Any drug dealer, smuggler, or cooker has to know the name Mateo Garcia. The problem is, we don't have a clue who or what department is on the take. I agree with Bleu. We need to get the FBI involved immediately, and they can interact with the Federales. Between the two agencies, they probably know who in Mexico is legit and who turns a blind eye to the drug gangs. There could be a snitch within the Federales who tipped Mateo off and the FBI needs to find out who they can and can't trust. They have to be assertive and let the Mexican authorities know that the missing American police detective and his seventy-year-old mother are in harm's way. That news is going to be splattered all over American and Mexican televisions, and I guarantee you it won't look good for any of them south of the border if they don't cooperate fully." Royce looked from face to face. "Are we all in agreement to call the FBI right now and suggest they take on this case as soon as humanly possible?"

Everyone nodded. It was time to make the call.

Royce dialed the local FBI office, set the phone to Speaker, and after a few transfers, got through to the SAC— Special Agent in Charge—Ronald Fuller. After explaining the situation and the location where Mitch and Mary Cannon had gone missing, Fuller said that the FBI's International Violent Crimes Unit would take over, and the nearest attaché office to Playa del Carmen was in Mexico City. Their office would dispatch agents to the area and, along with the police and Federales, find out who were the likely suspects and go from there. Royce rattled off Luis and Mateo's full names but said he didn't know who Mateo's contacts in Mexico were.

"I'll make the contact for you, Sergeant Royce. Email everything you have on both men to the attention of SAC David Camden. I'll make that call immediately and pass on the details that you've just told me. The teams working in Mexico know who the players are and without a doubt can connect and locate the men who had their hands in the kidnapping. This is something they'll act on right away. The drug gangs and kidnappers in Mexico are a vicious bunch, and I won't try to diminish the urgency of finding Detective Cannon and his mother. Time is of the essence."

"Thank you, Agent Fuller. I'll send a zipped file to Agent Camden's email address right away. He should expect it in his in-box in less than fifteen minutes."

Royce hung up, swirled his finger above his head, and yelled for everyone to get every file the PD had on Luis and Mateo ready to email. He needed it yesterday.

Chapter 33

I sat awake all night. My shaking wasn't only because of the cold but also from the snapping twigs I heard, and each one seemed closer than the one before. If I was cold and afraid, I knew my mom was far worse. She was slender and had on shorts and a thin yellow top. There wasn't a damn thing she could do to stay warm unless she balled up to keep her body heat close to her core. I heard her moans throughout the night and knew she was uncomfortable, yet there was no way for me to know whether she'd fallen asleep, and I didn't want to wake her if she had.

My mind was filled with thoughts about Mateo and his intentions for us. A US police detective was worth something, and he would take advantage of that. I was sure of it. Killing us without somehow lining his pockets wasn't Mateo's way. He'd been locked up for two years—not long but long enough to lose his top position in the drug trade industry coming in from Central America, moving through Mexico, and then into the United States. He needed to reestablish himself as a drug kingpin, a dangerous leader, and a menace to mankind wherever he went. Money and threats of killing an American cop and his mother would definitely make that happen. If there was any saving grace, it was that Mateo wouldn't kill us until he got whatever it was he wanted.

I heard Mom stir. "Are you awake, Mom?"

"Yes, honey. I can't sleep more than a few minutes at a time. I'm so cold, and I'm afraid of bugs and snakes crawling on us."

Besides venomous snakes, which I was sure were plentiful, there were far more dangerous animals lurking in the dark. I had no idea whether animals could smell fear, but I prayed that they couldn't.

"It'll be light in an hour or so and get warmer as the sun filters through the trees. We'll be able to see each other and everything around us too."

She sighed. "That'll be a relief. After that, the only other animal to fear is of the human variety."

I needed to say something to reassure her, and even if Mateo did demand money for our safe return, his word meant nothing, and it never had. Even so, I had to stay optimistic for her sake.

"I'm thinking he's holding us for ransom. I bet the Savannah PD already knows what's going on and has contacted the authorities. If Mateo has demanded money in exchange for our release, the FBI is likely already involved."

"Well, I hope we don't have to endure another night out here, and as much as I've prayed for our lives, I know God will protect us."

"I hope you're right, and I hope somebody is already looking for us. Why don't you lie down on the platform and curl up as tight as you can? That should warm you up a little."

"Okay, I'll try that."

Snapping sounds moved through the tangle of the jungle's vegetation and caught my ear. Originally farther out, the sound was closing in. Whatever it was had weight to it.

"Mitch?"

The hair stood up on the back of my neck. "Shh. Don't make a peep, Mom," I whispered. I patted the ground until I felt a fallen branch. I knew picking it up would alert whatever was coming our way, but I had to find something to use as a weapon if I needed it. "Mom, if you can find a limb or something to swat with, grab it now. Something long and heavy that you can handle. Whatever was coming this way is getting too close."

"Mitch, I'm afraid."

"I am, too, but our only choice is to protect ourselves."

Whatever was headed our way was only twenty feet or so from me. I was thankful it was approaching on my side of the platform and not Mom's. I listened for that low growl so I would know what I was up against, but instead, I heard snorting. I assumed it was a wild pig, which I would gladly deal with over a panther any day, yet a pig could be dangerous as well.

I sat motionless and tried to adjust my eyes and learn its location. I would swat at any movement in the bushes and hope to scare it off. The snorting intensified, and the swift movement caught me off guard. It was headed right for me, and I leapt to my feet and swung wildly. The branch in my hand connected with the animal. It squealed and ran into the jungle. I dropped to the ground, thankful that it ran away and we were fine.

"Mom, you okay?"

She was sobbing. "Is it gone, and what was it?"

"It ran off. I couldn't see it well, but I'm pretty sure it was a peccary, a wild pig, but the limb I swung hit its mark and scared it away. We're good for now. Just make sure to keep a big stick within reach at all times."

Chapter 34

The next morning, Royce sat in his office and stewed. It was his fault that Mitch and Mary had gone missing.

Kidnapped, asshole. Just say the word—kidnapped.

"Yeah, they were kidnapped, and I'm to blame."

Feeling that someone was staring at him, Royce looked up and saw Rue standing at his half-opened door. Rue poked his head in and glanced at the guest chairs then at Royce.

"You talking to yourself, Boss?"

"Yeah, I'm pissed and feeling pretty guilty. I've been here since six a.m. going over everything there is to know about Mateo Garcia."

Rue walked in and pointed at a guest chair. "May I?"

With a shrug, Royce told him to sit his ass down.

"So, pissed and guilty. I get the pissed part, but guilty of what?"

"It was me who told Mitch to take that stupid burner phone along and act like he was Luis. He had five days of paid vacation due him, yet I made him work during his mother's seventieth birthday cruise. If there's a real hell waiting for people, I deserve to be first in line."

Devon chuckled. "I'm pretty sure you'd have to be dead before you could get in line."

Royce swatted the air. "I'm so used to Mitch going along with whatever I suggest, I didn't even realize how selfish I was being. Mexico has police officers and the Federales. They could have easily taken care of the apprehension, and somebody right here at the precinct could have monitored that damn burner phone. It didn't have to be Mitch."

"I can't argue with you there, but what's done is done. Now, the FBI has to track them down and quick. People seem to disappear in those regions, and once that happens, it's damn near impossible to find them. The FBI and Federales better use every resource and snitch they have to locate Mitch and Mary fast."

"I'm going to Mexico."

"What? Why not give the FBI a minute to check for camera footage from the spot where the tours leave from, or even along the shops where the tourists flock, before you do something drastic like that? It won't take them more than a few hours to spot Mitch and Mary in the crowd if they were in that area."

Royce glanced at the clock—it was ten till eight. "If I don't hear anything by noon, I'm catching the next flight to Cancun."

"And how would you find Mitch if the FBI can't?"

"Don't worry. I'll work hand in hand with them. I'm not going rogue. Hell, I don't know a damn thing about the area, but I do know one thing."

Rue rubbed his forehead. "Yeah, and what's that?"

"I'm to blame, and that gives me a dog in the fight. Come hell or high water, I'm not returning to Savannah without a live and breathing Mitch and Mary Cannon."

Rue huffed. "Well, if that's the case, I'm going along."

"No you—"

Rue butted in. "Mitch is my partner, and he's saved my life before. It's the least I can do, and I really don't think you want to stop me. If you go, I go. End of story."

With a groan, Royce pushed back from his desk. "How did I end up with two stubborn detectives?"

Devon grinned. "We weren't stubborn until you became our boss."

Royce pointed his chin toward the door. "Come on. We have a morning meeting to attend. Bleu has updates he wants to share with everyone about the process the FBI in Mexico plans to use to find Mitch."

Rue raised his brows. "Good. Whatever it is, I hope they do it fast."

In the bullpen, the night and day shift teams gathered. Bleu called for everyone's attention and began.

"Last night, the FBI attaché in Mexico City was contacted about Mitch's disappearance. They're quite familiar with the heavy hitters in that area who target tourists to kidnap or sell drugs to. Personally, I'm confident that this was a targeted kidnapping, though, and the FBI agrees."

Royce glanced at Rue and nodded.

"Their Mexico City office is the closest one to Playa del Carmen, where Mitch and Mary disembarked the ship. There's a US Embassy consular office right in Playa del

Carmen, too, so it's a good place to set up a temporary FBI base. The latest news is that their team has arrived in Playa del Carmen, and they'll be spending today trying to retrace Mitch's footsteps after he and Mary left the ship. Mitch's mom told his sister just before they disembarked that she was going to do some shopping before they headed out on the Mayan ruins tour. That means they didn't cancel the trip, yet they never met up with the tour guide to go on it. According to the locals in Playa del Carmen and the cruise ship personnel, that area of shopping isn't overly large, and if they were there, they shouldn't be hard to spot roaming from store to store. From the time they left the ship"—Bleu checked his notes—"to the time they were supposed to meet with the tour guide gave them an hour and a half to shop. In that amount of time, they could have been watched, followed, and then abducted just before they reached their tour guide's vehicle."

Rue took his turn. "If the area is always that crowded when the ships come in, then Mitch would have yelled out, fought back, something. There had to be a ruse or a threat to get them to cooperate."

Bleu agreed. "And that's probably exactly what happened. If the FBI is lucky and there are cameras along the route to the tour bus parking area, they should be able to see exactly what unfolded."

The meeting ended with that information but nothing else to ensure Mitch and Mary's safety.

Chapter 35

Royce was on pins and needles until the update call came in at 11:47. Mitch and Mary had been spotted on camera in the shopping district along the harbor. Marie had told Rue that Mary was wearing a yellow top and floral shorts. She was the easiest target to spot, then the cameras showed a man, who the authorities were pretty certain was Mitch, within a few feet of her at all times. That was all they had so far since they were watching the footage as it had played out yesterday in real time. They couldn't fast-forward through the videos since nobody knew when the abduction had taken place.

What the FBI had passed on was that Mary carried a few bags, likely gifts, and she and Mitch had stopped for a beverage then continued on through the shops. They had another full hour before they had to make their way to the parking lot.

Until someone in the crowd matching what the FBI had in their database showed up on camera, they couldn't say with one hundred percent certainty which group in the area carried out the abduction.

As he sat in his office, Royce continued going through the

list of Mateo's known associates in the US, but he didn't know who the players were in Mexico. He would have to leave that in the hands of the FBI.

Rue knocked on Royce's door at noon—Royce's time limit for getting information.

"Well?"

"I just received an update and was about to let you know. Have a seat."

Rue eagerly sat down and leaned forward. "I hope it's good news."

Royce shrugged. "It's news, not good or bad, just an update. Mary and Mitch were spotted popping in and out of the shops just beyond the beachfront hotels. I guess that's where all the tourists go once they leave the ship."

"Uh-huh."

"That's all they have for now. I guess there's just under an hour left to watch on the videos before Mitch and Mary were due at the tour guide's vehicle. Anything could have happened during that time, and the next forty-five minutes or so should tell the story. The FBI knows the different gangs and drug cartels, and hopefully, they would recognize a few faces if they were caught on camera."

"Then we'd know without a shadow of a doubt who abducted Mitch and whether they were associates of Mateo's or not."

"At this point, I'm almost hoping they are. At least we know something about him. Anyone else is just a guessing game."

Rue waved away Royce's comment. "It had to be Mateo's

people. Nobody else knows who Mitch is. Why grab him instead of any other tourist?"

"Good point, Devon."

"So?"

"So, I'll give them until the time Mitch and Mary were supposed to meet the tour guide. The abduction had to have taken place before one o'clock."

"Do we know anything about Mateo's Mexican connections?"

"No, but I bet I know who does."

"Luis?"

"Yep, I'll contact his attorney right now."

Rue sat quietly while Royce made the call. Within minutes, a meeting had been set up, and the attorney said he would arrive at the precinct by twelve thirty. Royce would conduct the interview with Luis and hope to get names of people south of the border.

"We need some kind of a hook or bargaining chip," Rue said after Royce hung up. "Luis already made it clear he wasn't telling us anything more. He gave us Mateo's location in Mexico, but that's all."

"So we push even harder. I'll bs my way through the interview and say that the judge is going to throw the proverbial book at him. Mateo is MIA, not in the custody of the US judicial system, so Luis will bear all the responsibility of the three murders. I'll inform him that Colorado is off the table, which he'll be relieved to hear. And then I'll say that after he's convicted of the murders, he'll go directly to GDCP."

Rue chuckled. "He'll have no idea what that stands for."

"Oh, don't worry about that. I'll spell it out in detail—Georgia Diagnostic and Classification State Prison—where death row prisoners are housed until their execution. That ought to get his attention. Want to join me?"

"Hell yeah. We'll get him to spill the frijoles one way or another."

Royce laughed. "That was pretty clever if I do say so myself."

Royce called the jail guard and said that Luis's attorney was on his way. He added that Luis needed to be secured in the first interrogation room and that he and Rue would be right down. The meeting would be short and to the point. Give up names of their Mexican connections or go to death row. There wouldn't be an in-between or negotiations on the table.

They entered the interrogation room, where Luis already sat. His attorney was going through the check-in process and would join them any minute.

"Now what? I told you everything I had to say."

Royce held up his hands. "Nice try. There isn't going to be communication between us until your attorney is present, so zip it."

Luis grumbled then stared at the table. The doorknob turned, and the court-appointed attorney, Ross Silverman, walked in. He gave Rue and Royce an obligatory nod then took a seat next to Luis.

"So to what do I owe the pleasure of your company?" He glanced at Luis. "And his?"

"New details have come up since we last spoke with you.

You're well aware that Ms. Lopez and her teenaged children have succumbed to their gunshot wounds."

"I'm aware, and the gun wasn't in my client's hand, so why am I here?"

"Luis is taking the rap for Mateo, so the gun may as well have been in his hand." Royce looked into Luis's eyes. "Things have changed, buddy."

"Hey, talk to me, not him."

Royce held his stare. "Things have changed for Mr. Ortega."

"In what way?"

"As to where he's going to spend life. He won't be going to Colorado after all."

Silverman smiled and patted Luis's arm. "That's good news. You've been spared the worst prison in America. No Florence for you."

Royce chuckled. "Nope, he'll be housed at GDCP instead."

Silverman's face went pale.

"What is GDCP?" Luis asked.

The attorney coughed into his hand.

Royce spoke for him. "Seems like the cat's got your attorney's tongue. GDCP is where death row inmates spend their last days before they get the lethal injection. Strapped down to the table, can't move, allowed a few final words to your loved ones, but nobody will hear them because you don't have any loved ones. That's what GDCP is. Nice and cozy."

"You can't—"

"We can, and we did. The judge who will be hearing your case and I go way back. We were college roommates. What a stroke of luck, but then there is the judicial system, and since Georgia is a death sentence state, well, it is what it is."

Silverman whispered into Luis's ear. They had a few back-and-forth exchanges before the attorney addressed Royce.

"What do you want, and what's on the table?"

"There's only one thing on the table, and that's Mateo Garcia. If he's captured and extradited to the US, then Luis is off the death penalty hook. The only way that's going to happen is with names of known accomplices in Mexico. I don't want generic names either. I want the gang names, who the top dogs are, and where they're based. Without detailed information, there's no deal. Take it or leave it, but I guarantee you, you'll be dead whether you go to Florence or GDCP unless you give us Mateo and his Mexican associates. You've got five minutes, and your time starts now."

Chapter 36

"Doing okay, Mom? It's finally warmed up out here."

"Yes, but I keep wondering when those men are coming back."

"Don't know, but short of being hungry and thirsty, I'd like it better if they never returned."

I noticed her smile—that was a good thing. "I'd have to agree with that." She returned her focus to the numerous bug bites on her arms and legs.

I pointed my chin at her water bottle. "How much is left in there?"

"About half."

"Good. Drink it sparingly. I've been looking around to see if I can spot something edible, but honestly, I have no idea what's edible in the jungle."

"We should be more concerned about escaping."

"Escaping? We're chained to trees, Mom."

"So break the chain. I raised you kids to think on your feet. It's daylight, the men haven't returned yet, and it's the best time to try. Find a big rock and start hammering at the links."

"Okay, I think. First, I have to find a rock that'll work."

"There's one over here that would do."

"Can you reach it and toss it to me?"

Mom's grunting told me the rock was likely half buried in the jungle floor or far larger than she had thought.

"Can you get it or not?"

"I'm working on it, but I can't get it loose."

"Try using the stick I told you to keep close by."

"Okay. I'm prying it up, and it seems to be working now."

I looked around as I waited but didn't see anything around me that would work. I was depending on Mom, although I doubted that a rock could break a chain, especially limestone, which was plentiful in the area. As it was, we had nothing but time to try.

"I got it, Mitch!"

"Great. Now pick it up, come as close to me as you can, and then just roll it my way. Don't toss it, or it might bounce out of my reach."

Mom did as instructed. The rock was a decent-sized piece of limestone, about twice the size of my fist, but limestone was brittle and often crumbled. I would give it everything I had, though, and try.

I pulled on the chain until it was taut then began striking it with the rock. I was immediately let down when the limestone cracked. It was half the size it was before. "This won't work, Mom. Maybe if it was granite, it would, but limestone is too sandy and brittle. Good idea, though, so let's keep thinking about what might work."

For the next half hour, I checked out everything as far as

my chain could reach. I thought about the platform and what Mateo had said—that the area used to be much larger with more processing stations but was eventually discovered, torn down, and whatever was left had given way to the jungle environment. There had to be something there—nails, pieces of steel, whatever they'd used to build the original cocaine plant in the jungle.

I gave the platform a hard look, then I saw them. Several long spikes on the underside held the timbers together. There was a chance that I could put a link over the spike and pull until it stretched and opened. I opted for the link closest to my zip tie and used my body weight as leverage.

Mom watched and whispered prayers for my success. With the link over the spike where it connected, I pulled with all my might, and the link began to stretch and open. All I needed was to stretch it far enough to slip the zip tie out and I would be free.

"Mom, it's working. I'll be out of here in no time, and then we'll find a way to get you free. Look under the platform for the closest spike to you. There has to be some on your side too."

It took five more minutes before I was able to slip my zip tie through the sliver of an opening I had made by stretching the chain's link.

"I'm out. Now we need to get you out too." I ran to my mother's side, gave her an enormous hug, and got busy. There was no way in hell I would waste the time I'd spent freeing myself just to be recaptured and chained up again. "Let's see what we have over here."

"I spotted a spike right by the platform's end." Mom pointed, and I headed to that spot.

The only problem was her strength. I wondered if she was strong enough to stretch a link open and slip out like I'd done. She walked with me to the platform's end.

"Here's what you have to do, and we have no time to waste. You have to pull with all your might if you want to get loose."

"Yes, I will. Just get me set up."

I smiled. There was that woman who had always been a force in our family. "Okay, sit down about two feet from the side of the platform and face it. I'll hook a link around that spike, then you brace your feet against the platform and pull with every ounce of strength you have."

"Got it." She looked around and nodded. "Hurry, Mitch. We have no idea when they'll return."

The chain's link I'd secured was about three feet from my mom. She would have to settle for that length of chain remaining attached to her zip tie, but it wasn't the end of the world. She needed enough room to use her legs as leverage.

"Okay, give it everything you've got and pull like hell."

I stayed beside the link and watched. It was beginning to stretch. Hers would have to stretch a little more than mine had since the opening would have to be wide enough to separate that link from the one next to it.

"It's stretching. Keep it up, Mom, and you'll be out of there in seconds."

She pulled even harder. Her face was strained and turning red. The veins bulged on her forehead, and I worried that she might have a heart attack, but she was a fighter and in generally good health.

"You're almost there. Do you need a break?"

"No, I need to get this damn thing off of me."

I chuckled. My mom wasn't one to swear often. "A couple more hard pulls and the opening will be wide enough."

She grunted and pulled again, then it was done.

"Okay, stop. We've got it! I just have to slip that link out of the one next to it, and then we're out of here. We need to get as far away from this spot as possible and find help."

She was free. One more quick embrace, then we grabbed our water bottles and headed down the trail we had come in on.

Mom looked worried. "What if we run into them?"

"We won't stay on the path very long. The plan is to walk parallel to the driveway we came in on but deep enough in the jungle where we won't be seen if they return. That's the only way I know that'll lead us back to civilization."

Chapter 37

Royce grabbed the receiver of his ringing phone and answered the call. More news was coming in from Mexico's temporary FBI office in Playa del Carmen. It was just before one o'clock, and he anxiously jotted down notes as he listened to SSA Camden, the agent in charge of the investigation, share his latest update. Royce set his phone to Speaker and, with his office door closed, was sure to have no interruptions.

"Tell me everything you know so far, Agent Camden."

"Dave is fine. No formalities necessary, Sergeant Royce."

"If that's the case, then you can call me Raleigh. So, did you see the abduction?"

"We believe so, although it was very discreet and slick. Nobody would be the wiser, and I'm sure Detective Cannon and his mother weren't even aware they were being kidnapped."

"How is that possible?"

We saw the mother being approached by a man holding a sign just like the ones the private tour guides use. By using the camera footage from the last store, we followed them to the vehicle he directed her to, and she climbed in."

"You're saying *she*. Where was Mitch?"

"We went back to the earlier footage, right at the same time the man approached Mrs. Cannon, and looked around. We didn't see Detective Cannon near her, but she was just coming out of the ladies' room."

"So they were already watching her?"

"It looks that way. Mitch might have been in the men's room at that time. We did catch him a few minutes later. He was standing at the ladies' room as if waiting for his mother to come out."

"So they missed each other, Mary went with the stranger she thought was their driver, and then did you see Mitch at all after that?"

"We did. We went back to watching the footage at the parking lot. Minutes later, Mitch appeared on the screen, said a few words to the driver and his mom, then climbed into the SUV. A second man then opened the passenger-side door and got in. The vehicle headed south out of the lot as if it was going toward Tulum."

"Plates, IDs, a vehicle make and model? Tell me you have something."

"Only that the vehicle was a black SUV. Our software program is trying to get a match to the man who led Mrs. Cannon to the vehicle. Down here, outside the big cities, the internet service comes in and out in waves. It's far less reliable and shuts down every so often."

"So nobody recognized the man just by seeing his face?"

"The distance was too far, Raleigh, and the same went for the second guy, too, but if we get a facial match with the software, we'll be in business."

Royce groaned, thanked Dave, and asked him to keep him updated. A knock sounded on his door just as he ended the call. Royce yelled out to come in, and Rue stepped into his office.

"Any news?"

"Yeah, and it isn't helpful. It's time we book two flights to Cancun, Mexico."

"And you have that list from Luis we can work on during the flight?"

"Damn right I do. We're going in and finding Mitch and Mary whether we have help from the FBI or not. I need to call Riley and Bleu, have them overlap shifts and have their guys put in some OT, and you need to get all your ducks in a row. If I score a couple of empty seats, we'll be flying out later today. We're taking along our weapons, and I'll clear that with TSA, but we're going in as tourists so we blend in with the crowd and don't attract any attention. Leave here at four, go home, grab your passport, and pack your tropical clothes."

Rue huffed before walking out. "Like I even own any. Should I update Marie before we go?"

Royce leaned back and stared at the ceiling before answering. "Just tell her that the FBI spotted them on store cameras and we're going in to help track them down. That's all you need to say, and essentially, that's all we have anyway."

"Roger that."

Chapter 38

We'd gotten as close to the dirt path as I dared. Through the thick jungle growth, I could see the clearing in the brush from the driveway, and I would hear any vehicle that approached. What I didn't know was how long we'd been on that narrow path before Cruz had stopped the vehicle— Mom and I were both dozing at the time. I also had no idea what the roads were like before we turned off onto that isolated driveway. I remembered that the main road going south to Tulum was 307, a busy modern federal highway. What I didn't know was if we'd turned directly off that highway onto the driveway or if Cruz had taken a number of side roads to end up there.

All I could do was keep a road within sight so we didn't get lost in the jungle, and pray that a passerby wasn't Mateo or one of his men. I wasn't sure how we could make it to safety since I had no idea how many men were on Mateo's payroll and who they were. I might approach someone, thinking they would help us, then find out the person was one of his men. The smartest thing I could do was find civilization and call the authorities. We needed changes of clothes, too, to hide our appearances. The best I could do was continue on at Mom's pace and try to find help somewhere once nighttime took over. It would be easier to hide from Mateo and his men under the cover of darkness.

I checked the time—just after three. The sun would set in three and a half hours, but the jungle would darken long before that. We had several hours of daylight left, then I needed to find a safe spot for us to spend the night without the threat of jungle animals getting too close. I saw a downed log and decided we needed a ten-minute break. We had been walking for several hours, and no matter what, I had to keep Mom's age in mind. Just because I was capable of continuing on didn't mean she was.

"Let's sit for a few minutes and drink a little water. Are you getting worn out?"

"Some, but not enough to stop looking for help. So what happens to our things that were left on the ship?"

I shrugged. "I have no idea. I'm sure they'll set everything aside and hope we'll reappear to claim it in Tampa."

"They aren't responsible for our disappearance, are they?"

"I don't think so. If anybody takes the time to read the fine print when they disembark, I'm sure there's some verbiage that says the cruise ship isn't responsible for the guests once they're on dry ground."

Mom took a gulp of water. She looked around. "I think people eat ferns in salads, don't they?"

"Yeah, but I don't know what kind of ferns these are. We can probably eat beetles." I grinned when she feigned gagging. "Ready to keep going?"

"Yep, as ready as I'll ever be."

We stood, and I heard a vehicle coming down the path. I ducked, pulled Mom down, and put my finger to my mouth. I whispered for her not to make a sound. With lightning speed, I mentally calculated how long it would take for Mateo's men to track us down. We'd been walking at a slow pace because of Mom, but depending on how many men were in that vehicle and how fast they could plow through the jungle, they could catch up to us in less than an hour—and long before nightfall.

Once the vehicle passed, I figured it would take another ten minutes to reach the end of the road and then twenty minutes to reach the platform. Even including that amount of time, and with Mateo screaming out orders, they could still find us before dark. We needed to move and move fast. We weren't going to make it to a main road, and once they realized we'd escaped, Mateo would definitely have more men come in and station themselves along the roadways in case we popped out of the jungle. Before dark, we needed to find a place to hide. As it stood, we were on the run with no idea of where to go or whom to trust.

"Mom, we need to look for a pile of boulders to hide behind, an outcropping to back up to where we'll be safe from predators, or downed logs we can lie under. Let's keep an eye out for anything like that as we move along."

She nodded and continued on as she grasped my hand tightly. I heard her strained breathing and knew the increased pace was taking a toll. We needed to find a place to hunker down where we wouldn't be seen or harmed by man or animal.

"This way. I think I see something that might work."

I'd found a dugout spot, not really a cave but more like a shelter used by an animal at some point. It looked abandoned, as if whatever had previously used it moved on. There weren't any fresh tracks or evidence of an animal being there recently, and by squeezing together, we could both fit into the burrow and stay warm throughout the night—if we weren't discovered.

"Mom, if you need to use the bathroom, then do it now. Once we're in place in that dugout, we're staying put. We don't have a choice. I'm not trying to scare you, but you know the consequences. If Mateo or his men find us, we're as good as dead."

With a stiff upper lip, Mom disappeared behind a cluster of bushes, and I did the same. I hadn't heard any voices yet, but I was certain it wouldn't be long before we did.

Back at the dugout, I had Mom climb inside, get as comfortable as she could for the duration, and confirm that she was set. She said she was.

I looked around. "I'll be right back."

"Where the hell are you going, Mitch? Don't you dare leave me here!"

"Shh… I'm not leaving you. I'm only going about fifty feet away to tear up a bunch of greenery and grab limbs. We need to be camouflaged behind that hole we'll be staying in, and once I'm in place, I'm going to cover the entrance so we blend in with the jungle."

"So we'll be safe and go unnoticed?"

"That's the plan, and even if they get close, as long as we

don't move a muscle, they won't have a clue we're here."

I gathered the limbs, crawled in, then layered them and the leaves over us. Danger was right around the corner, but as long as we remained still, I hoped for the best. We were in for a long night, and I had no idea what tomorrow would bring.

Mom turned to me and whispered, "Honey?"

"Yeah?"

"We need to pray for our lives."

I nodded. "I know, and we also need to pray for darkness to come soon."

Chapter 39

They booked two tickets for the last flight of the day to Cancun, Mexico. The only seats available were in first class, which wasn't a bad option, just expensive.

Devon picked up Royce at five o'clock, and they headed to the airport, each with a suitcase with their sidearm stowed inside. Everything was taken care of at the precinct, and the other sergeants had a firm grip on the department's personnel and duties for as long as it took to bring Mitch and Mary home. Bleu and Riley wished Royce and Rue safe travels and good luck in finding them.

Later, as they sat on the airplane and waited for takeoff, Rue stared out the window, said a silent prayer for a safe flight, and wondered what Mitch was doing. Rue wasn't sure he actually wanted to know. Mateo's men, according to the names Luis had given them, were ruthless and dangerous. They wouldn't hesitate to kill anyone who got in their way or threatened their drug enterprise. On Mateo's go, they would shoot and kill even a seventy-year-old woman without flinching.

The runway, the ground, and finally the buildings

disappeared from sight as the plane climbed into the clouds. Within minutes, they were over open water and en route to Cancun, Mexico. The flight would take several hours. Then they planned to rent a car to go to Playa del Carmen. Flying into Cancun was the most direct and fastest route.

As they flew, Royce and Rue studied the arrests and convictions of each person Luis had named as one of Mateo's henchmen in Mexico. If he was indeed calling the shots in Mitch and Mary's disappearance, they wouldn't last long at the hands of those monsters.

Rue leaned toward Royce and kept his voice down. Even though they were in first class with only two seats side by side, they still didn't want anyone to overhear their conversation.

"What do you think Mateo's motivation is if he's behind this? We don't have absolute assurance it's him or his men since nobody recognized the driver considering the distance they were from store cameras."

"I guaran-damn-tee you Mateo is calling the shots. Somehow, those men knew Mitch and Mary were on the ship and that they had a tour planned in the afternoon. They staged the scene with that sign, followed them through the marketplace, and waited for the perfect opportunity to swoop in and get Mary alone. I don't know how bad the blood is between Mitch and Mateo, but it shouldn't be bad enough to kill over. Maybe they're holding them for ransom."

Rue wrinkled his face. "Wouldn't they have called us by now?"

With a groan, Royce continued. "Honestly, I don't know shit about the tactics Mexicans use with hostages and ransom demands. I've never had to deal with it. One thing I do know, though, is that ransom demands don't often go well for the hostages."

The sky darkened, and that meant a second night that Mitch and Mary could be held in some remote location that only the kidnappers knew about.

Devon shook his head as he stared out at the last glow as the sun dropped beneath the horizon. "I hope Mary's getting through this without too much trouble."

"Mitch will protect her at all costs. You can count on that. Try to catch a nap, Devon. We've got a long night ahead of us."

Later, Rue felt his head bob. He dozed off, then the sound of the landing gear being lowered woke him. They had both fallen asleep, and it was apparent by the lights coming on that they were on the final approach to Cancun.

Royce rubbed his eyes, sat up straight, and opened his seat belt. "I'll be right back. I need to use the restroom before we have to buckle in for the duration."

Rue peered out the window at the approaching lights. From the sky, Cancun was well-lit, and he knew its reputation as a hot spot where people stayed up all night. He'd never been there before, and neither had Royce or Mitch, but under different circumstances, he was sure it could be fun.

He thought about what they had to accomplish that night.

We need to meet up with the FBI when we reach Playa, find out what they've learned since Royce spoke with them last, and go from there. We'll compare notes and see if their list of Mateo's amigos matches the names given to us by Luis.

Minutes later, Royce sat down and buckled up. "What a view out there, huh?"

"Yeah. I sure hope Mitch and Mary are in some remote spot near Playa del Carmen. In a city this big"—he pointed out the window—"we'd never find them."

"Keep the faith, Rue. As soon as we reach Playa del Carmen, we're going to find out everything there is to know about Mateo Garcia and his gang of outlaws south of the border. There's no quitting until Mitch and Mary are on a plane with us, heading back to the United States. For now, I hope getting through customs is a breeze and the car rental goes without a hitch."

The jet landed and taxied to the terminal. There were perks of being in first class—they exited the plane within a minute of the door opening. After a half hour in line to get through customs, Royce secured the rental car, and they left. Heading south toward Playa del Carmen, they would reach the city within an hour.

Royce turned to Rue. "Call Dave Camden and let him know we're on our way. We'll meet with them tonight and be ready to hit the ground running first thing in the morning."

"Roger that, Boss."

Chapter 40

It was after ten o'clock by the time Royce and Rue passed the sign showing they had reached Playa del Carmen.

Royce let out a long sigh. "We're finally here. It's been a long day, and now we have to find the hotel that everyone's staying at."

Rue checked his cell phone's notepad. "We'll be at the Mayan Paradise. It's along the beach." Rue pointed at the road sign that indicated the beach hotels were to the left. "Go that way."

"Got it."

"I imagine we'll see it as we drive. The closest hotels to the water are along Avenida 1 Norte." Rue pointed again. "I see the sign. It's the third hotel on the right."

Royce turned in and found a parking spot near the rear of the building. "These waterfront hotels must be popular. They're all packed. Lucky we found a spot."

"And lucky we found two rooms. Looks like Dave is in room 607."

"Humph. I bet he has a good view."

They unloaded their bags and headed to the front

entrance. Just beyond the foyer was the concierge and reservations counter. Although they weren't there to enjoy the amenities, the hotel looked gorgeous. Marble walls and floors along with tropical plants and Mayan décor provided a stunning ambience.

Rue whispered as they approached the reservations counter. "Who's paying for this?"

"Unfortunately, the taxpayers of Savannah, which includes us too. I'm putting it on my precinct's stipend card."

"Okay. Should I call Dave and tell him we'll be right up?"

"Yeah, go ahead while I get us checked in."

Rue stepped aside and took a seat in the conversation pit to the right of the entry.

Minutes later, Royce approached Rue while pulling both suitcases behind him.

Devon glanced his way. "Oh, sorry about that. Dave said we should meet them on the deck out back."

Royce nodded. "Let's get rid of these suitcases first. We're in rooms 406 and 408."

"Sounds good. I hope we're facing the water."

Royce said they were, although they would be spending little time at the hotel. They reached their rooms, dropped off their bags, then with the folder of names from Luis, boarded the elevator to the first floor and followed the signs to the deck.

Outside, with the Caribbean Sea directly across the beach, the view—even in the dark—was stunning. Waves lapped the shoreline, and the sound of people still on the beach wafted up to the hotel's deck.

Although Royce and Rue had never met any of the agents in person, they knew where to go. Off to their left was a large table with a handful of men sitting around it. A man called out to Royce and waved.

Royce jerked his chin in their direction. "Apparently, that's them. Hopefully, they have new information to share."

At the table, names and ranks were exchanged. Two Federales were among the group, one being Pedro Torres, whom Juan Ramirez from SVU had spoken with over the phone a day earlier. The other was Dario Fuentes.

Royce and Rue took the empty seats and listened as Dave Camden explained where they were in the investigation. They still hadn't identified either man at the black SUV that Mitch and Mary had climbed into, but they did know the names of most of the players who were part of Mateo's posse. The nine men had served time in the Mexican jail system, and out of those nine, three were being watched by the local police, who had nothing unusual to report. As of that day, the FBI and Federales hadn't tracked down the others or Mateo Garcia.

"We don't know where they're holed up," Dave said, "but we're pretty sure that they're the ones who initiated the kidnapping."

"What about homes, relatives, or vehicles in their names? Wouldn't you get a better idea of their whereabouts by tracking down that information?"

"Yes, we would, but *familia* in Mexico is very tight. Nobody talks about anyone, and none of the criminals have vehicles registered in their own names. They borrow, rent, or steal cars in order to stay under the radar."

"Can we have a look at the names you've gathered? We were given names by Mateo's right-hand man in the States. Some may be duplicates and some may not, but we need to compare them anyway."

"Absolutely." Dave opened his folder, and side by side, he and Royce looked at each name. With his pen, Dave circled two names that weren't on his or the Federales' lists. "Humph. I wonder who Cruz Montoya and Elan Sanchez are. Neither are in our books." Dave turned to Pedro. "Do you recognize those names?"

"No, never heard of either, but I'm not surprised. The most trustworthy amigos don't participate in the everyday tasks with the others. They don't often get popped. That means those two are the most valuable to Mateo. The name Alejandro Nunez is on both lists, though. We should start with him. Between you, us, and the Playa del Carmen police commander, Roberto DeLeon, we should be able to track him down."

"Good, and what about these two characters, Elan and Cruz?" Royce asked.

Dave grinned. "We find them, we find Mateo Garcia. We'll push hard on that first thing in the morning. Right now, at this time of night, there's nothing except bars open, and nobody will talk to us anyway."

Rue took his turn. "Maybe one of them is linked to that black SUV."

"Possibly. We'll find out everything we can about both of them as soon as the police commander gets to work in the morning. He's got to know somebody who knows somebody else who can help us. For now, I'd suggest calling it a night. Let's all meet in the dining room at eight a.m., have breakfast, and then get started. Tomorrow is going to be a fact-finding day."

Chapter 41

"How are you doing, Mom?"

"That depends on if you want the truth or what you want to hear."

I let out a quiet chuckle. "I guess that was a stupid question. I haven't heard a voice in hours. That was pretty scary earlier when Mateo and his men were close by, but I think they've left for the night. There's no way they can find us in the dark."

"Unless they have plenty of flashlights."

I flicked a mosquito off my cheek. "Yeah, or that. I bet you're starving."

"We're both starving, Mitch. Without food or water, we'll die, and if they catch us, we'll die."

"But if we find a way out of here, we won't. The question is, do we risk walking that path at night and hope there isn't a vehicle sitting with its lights off, just waiting for us to come out of the jungle, or do we wait until morning so we can see them if they're out there?"

"The jungle animals are more active at night, right?"

"Maybe, but I'm no expert on that. I did see something

earlier when I was gathering leaves and branches that caught my attention, though."

"Yeah, what? A car with the keys in the ignition?"

I shook my head. "If nothing else, you still have your sarcastic sense of humor."

"Gotta do something so we don't go crazy. Anyway, what did you see?"

"In college, I used to have a Mexican buddy whose mom made tree spinach."

"What the heck is that?"

"Well, I didn't see it firsthand, but back then, he showed us pictures from a trip he took to the Yucatan, where his family was from. I guess they call it chaya there, and it's a popular Mayan dish. The leaves can be prepared any way spinach is, and the broth can also be used as tea. There's one problem, though. There are stinging hairs on the wild variety, and it's toxic if eaten raw in large quantities."

"Then what's the upside?"

"We can eat a few leaves at a time for nourishment, and I believe I saw some about thirty feet out. I'm going to double-check that in the morning. It's something, and at this point, we really do need to eat."

Mom lifted her water bottle. "I can't see what's left in here, but it feels like it'll be empty by tomorrow."

"Yeah, mine, too, but those leaves might help."

Mom squirmed. "My legs are cramping. Do you think it's safe to climb out for a few minutes? I have to pee again too."

I was hesitant. I had no idea what the mindset of those men was. Did they leave and vow to find us tomorrow, or were they sitting in the dark and waiting for us to make a risky move that could end our lives? I didn't know.

"I hate to say this, but it's too dangerous to go out. We have no idea if they're out there just waiting for us to do something. For all we know, they could be sitting in the dark twenty feet away."

"Just the thought of that gives me goose bumps," Mom whispered.

"Yeah, me too. I'll do everything in my power to get us out of here tomorrow. I promise you that."

She squeezed my hand. "At least I'm not cold."

We remained in our burrow, and as Mom restlessly slept, I kept an ear perked for sounds outside our hiding spot. I was sure I could tell the difference between people and animals walking, and people—especially Mateo's thugs—definitely wouldn't be as quiet and stealthy as a panther hunting its prey. As I sat there, I did pray. Tomorrow, we would get away or be captured. There was no other option. As days passed, we would become weaker and weaker until we died of hunger and thirst. We had to make our move at daybreak and hope that whoever we saw or whatever home we came upon had a phone we could use to call for help.

I must have dozed at some point during the night. I woke to birds chirping and the daytime animals skittering about. Although I knew it was morning, the dense jungle was still an hour from daylight shining through. We couldn't take the chance of wandering out just yet. If Mateo and his men had spent the night out there, they would be stirring soon enough. As much as I wanted to put distance between us, I had to wait and see.

Chapter 42

The phone in Devon's room rang at seven fifteen. He rose from the balcony chair and answered it, already knowing who it was.

"Hello?"

"You up?"

"Yeah, I just got out of the shower, and now I'm in my bathrobe, drinking a cup of coffee on the balcony. It'll likely be the only chance I get to see what this area of the world is really like."

Royce huffed into the phone. "Believe me, if we're looking in every nook and cranny, rocks along the beaches, mangroves and jungles, you'll get your fill of the Yucatan Peninsula really fast."

"You're probably right. I sure hope we make headway today."

"We will. We have to for Mitch and Mary's sake. We aren't stopping until we hit the sheets tonight."

"Sounds good to me. I'll bang on your door in a half hour," Rue said.

As he stared out at the sea, Rue thought of the irony. A

beautiful view lay in front of him, but the crimes committed right under people's noses would shock them. Tourists lived in a bubble, believing that vacations were always safe and went perfectly. Even though he was a cop, Mitch had made that crucial mistake, too, and the FBI and police had no idea what had happened to him and his mother. They had no means of communicating with him. The kidnappers likely had taken his phone and turned it off.

Rue dressed, brushed his teeth, and left his room. Three steps later, he banged on Royce's door and was let in.

"Ready?"

"Yep, gotta grab the room key and the folder. Guess we're gathering at the Federales building on Calle 60 North. We'll just follow the others after breakfast."

"Good enough. Let's head down, eat, and save the shop talk for the privacy of the Feds' office."

Royce and Rue met with the four FBI agents and exchanged the typical morning courtesies. "How was your room? Did you sleep well? Do you have a water view?" Then they ordered breakfast. The drive to the Federales' Playa del Carmen office, according to Dave, would take fifteen minutes because of traffic.

Dave began the update even though Royce preferred to eat his food first then get down to business. Dave explained that he'd spoken that morning with Pedro Torres, who had already talked to the police commander, Roberto DeLeon. Commander DeLeon would join the group at the Federales office for the morning meeting and offer all the information he knew about the names in question. That was a positive start to the day.

"Let's eat and get the hell out of here," Dave said when the waitress carried a large tray to their table. "Mitch and his mom are counting on us."

By nine o'clock, the group had headed out with Royce and Rue following in their rental car. As Royce drove, Rue scratched out notes to discuss during the meeting.

Royce glanced over. "Whatcha writing?"

"To check and see if any of the men whose names we got from Luis has a black SUV. Also, we need to know more about Cruz, Elan, and Alejandro and if the commander has heard of any of them. We need to know where the drug busts took place that sent a half-dozen men to jail, and"—he looked at Royce—"anything else?"

"Yeah, who is still in jail and who isn't. Have you updated Marie since yesterday?"

"No. We don't really have any news."

Royce tipped his head at the phone lying on Rue's lap. "Call her anyway. Tell her we're here and that we hope to make a lot of progress today."

"On it." Rue dialed the number and set his phone to Speaker.

Marie picked up immediately. "Hi, Devon. Find out anything yet?"

"Not yet, and I have you on Speaker. Sergeant Royce and I are here, and we're following the FBI guys to the office of the Federales. We're hoping to break this case today and find Mitch and your mom. The police commander is joining us there too."

"Good. Mom thinks she's tough, but I can't imagine how she's getting through this."

"Mitch won't let anything happen to her, Marie," Rue said.

"I know he won't, but what—"

Devon interrupted. "Don't think negative thoughts. It'll only upset you more. We've got the FBI, Federales, local police, and the Savannah police working on this. We'll find them, I promise you."

Royce shot Rue a frown then shook his head.

Devon noticed but continued. "Okay, just wanted to give you a quick update. I'll call you back as soon as we know more."

"Have you tried Mitch or Mom's phones?"

"Yep. Mitch's is turned off, and we don't have Mary's number."

"Here, let me give it to you." Marie rattled off the number, then Rue jotted it down, ended the call, and pocketed his phone.

"Don't make promises you can't keep, Rue."

Devon's eyebrows shot up. "You've got to have faith, Boss. Without it, what do we have?"

"Facts. We have to work with facts. It's the only way to find Mitch and Mary."

Royce clicked his left blinker, waited for traffic to pass, then turned in to the parking lot behind Dave Camden. After parking next to Dave and exiting the car, they entered the building and passed through Security together. Dave took charge since it was apparent he was fluent in Spanish. Royce was thankful that the FBI team was since, left on their own, he and Rue wouldn't get very far.

"Right this way, guys. Pedro said that the police

commander has already arrived." Dave slapped his hands together. "Let's get down to business and make this a productive day."

Dave led them to an office full of cubicles and desks, and to the right sat a large table with several men already gathered around it. Dave made the introductions between Royce, Rue, and Commander DeLeon. After they all took seats, the meeting began.

Everyone took out their notes, and blank sheets of paper and pens were available at the center of the table.

Pedro Torres, the Federales leader in the investigation, asked for the names we'd been given by Luis Ortega. He read them off to the police commander, whose eyes widened when Alejandro Nunez's name came up.

"Yes, we're familiar with that man," Roberto said. "He was a lifelong associate of Mateo Garcia when Mateo lived in Mexico. Come to think of it, in the last week, Alejandro has made himself scarce. He was under surveillance for a few days because of a tip we received about illegal activities." He smiled. "We use confidential informants here in Mexico, too, but then Alejandro fell off our radar. He left his apartment Friday morning and hasn't been seen since. But why are you so sure that the kidnapping was carried out by Mateo Garcia and his men?"

Royce spoke up. "He and Mitch go way back, and the timing works out perfectly. Mateo was released from the US prison system, immediately killed three people, and is now back on Mexican soil and calling the shots. I'm sure that's why Alejandro is MIA. We need to track down Alejandro as well as those two characters, Cruz and Elan. So you do know where Alejandro lives?"

"Yes, but like I said, he hasn't returned home. He lives on the south side of Playa."

"Pull their phone records, then."

Pedro and Roberto laughed.

Royce frowned. "Did I say something funny?"

Pedro spoke up. "No, Sergeant Royce. It's just that things work differently here than they do in the States. To obtain phone records could take months. There isn't a system in place here that treats anything as an urgent situation. I'm sorry."

"Then can you at least access the motor vehicle records, type in their names, and see if any of them or their family members own a black SUV?"

"Certainly, we can do that."

They waited as Pedro tapped the keys of his laptop.

He let out a sigh. "Nothing under Alejandro Nunez."

"But if the city police were surveilling him, wouldn't they see him come and go?"

"Yes, we did," Roberto said, "but he was always picked up and dropped off."

"Then how about the person who picked him up and dropped him off? He likely took Alejandro to the place he's staying at now. You need to get him in front of us today."

"The man's clean. We've already checked to see if he has a criminal record," Pedro said.

Royce swatted the air. "Doesn't matter. Anyone can be questioned whether they have a record or not. We have to speak to him right away. Wherever Alejandro is, I bet my bottom dollar that Mateo is right alongside him."

"Okay, I'll send some officers to pick him up," Roberto said.

"I've got another idea," Rue said. "We had the warrants for the burner phones used between Luis and Mateo. I don't know if or how much Mateo used that phone for calling other people, but we can have our tech department access the text messages between Mitch and Mateo when Mateo thought he was Luis. They can pull up Mitch's back-and-forth texts with Mateo before that phone went dead. I doubt if it'll help us locate him, but there could be something helpful on there between them up to the point when Mitch was kidnapped."

Royce nodded. "Great idea, Devon. Call Tom now and put him on Speakerphone."

Rue dialed the tech department's number at the Habersham precinct and got Tom on the line. He asked the necessary questions about accessing the burner phone's text records, and Tom said there wouldn't be a problem. They still had all the information they needed at their fingertips, plus the warrant was still valid if they needed anything more.

"Great, and how soon can you get those texts over to us, say the ones from Thursday until the burner was shut off?"

"Within the hour."

Royce cut in. "That's perfect, Tom." He noticed that Pedro was the only one there with a laptop. "Send everything to Pedro Torres. He's the Federales commander in charge of the investigation. I'll have him give you his email address."

After Tom was told where to forward the text messages, the men got back to work.

"How about those other two guys, Elan and Cruz? Anything as far as vehicles or an address for either of them?"

Pedro tapped the keys again and looked up both names. "Nothing, and that's likely why nobody knows who they are. They've remained ghosts, and ghosts are in high demand, especially in the drug industry."

Rue raked his hair. "We need something else. You have to know where all the drug busts took place, right?"

"Yes. That information, we have," Pedro said.

Royce fist pumped the air. "Okay, now we're getting somewhere. Can you access that information now?"

"Certainly, but how far back should I go?"

"Mateo bolted from Mexico to avoid jail and came to the States in 2015. I'd say everything going back to 2014 for sure."

Seconds later, Pedro had pulled up the drug bust locations for the last eight years. "You want every drug bust or just the ones that involved Mateo's known acquaintances?"

Royce rubbed his forehead. "We have to start at the source— Mateo and his associates. Otherwise, we'll be looking at people and places that have no affiliation whatsoever with Mitch."

"Sure thing. Just one moment, Sergeant Royce." Pedro narrowed down his parameters and hit Enter. They waited for a minute while the system updated the results. "Here we go. There were seven drug busts during those years, and they are all within a fifty-mile radius of Playa."

"Great. Let's begin with the ones closest to town, check

them, and work our way out. Between all of us here, we can get that done today. We just need to organize our efforts."

"But what about the text messages your tech department was going to send me?" Pedro asked.

"Bring your laptop along," Royce said.

Rue took his turn. "How many of those seven locations were right in Playa del Carmen?"

Pedro scanned the screen. "Looks like there were two. We can knock them out in a half hour and then move on."

Royce pushed back his chair and stood. "Then let's saddle up. We've got to get through those seven locations, especially if they aren't all in buildings."

"They aren't, Sergeant Royce. Two of them were cocaine labs out in the jungle," Pedro said.

"Shit. Then we definitely need to check those two around noon when the sun is at its highest. Later in the day, it'll be too hard to see." Royce turned to Roberto. "Have your officers pick up that driver while we check out the buildings here in Playa. It's the fastest way to get things done. Have them contact you when they're heading in with him. We'll come back, ask what needs to be asked, and go from there. We still need to watch for those text messages to come in too."

Chapter 43

The sun had finally risen high enough to shine through the thick tree canopy. I cautiously moved a few limbs aside, peered from left to right, and didn't see anything that gave me pause. Over the last few hours, I'd listened closely and hadn't heard any voices or footsteps, and the jungle animals seemed to be in siesta mode too. The opportunity to keep moving had come, and we needed to go.

"Mom, why don't you use the bathroom while I go pick a handful of that chaya? We need some kind of nourishment to make it through the day."

"Okay. I won't go far, just thirty feet or so to the right."

"Sounds good, and no matter what, just be as quiet as possible."

"I will."

I headed to the area where I'd noticed the chaya yesterday and carefully watched my footsteps. As I moved slowly through the brush, I looked back once as Mom disappeared behind a large tree, then I continued on.

Now where exactly was that? Ah, there it is.

Once I reached the bush, I was careful to pull off the

leaves because of the stinging hairs. I folded the leaves and put them in my pants and shirt pockets. I was sure only a few leaves would hold us over for the day, and too many were toxic in the raw form anyway. Just as I was about to return to the burrow, I heard a gut-wrenching scream. Mom was yelling for help, and as I spun, I saw Cruz with a firm grip on her arm.

He called out, "Detective Cannon, come out from your hiding place right now, or your mother will die. You've got ten seconds."

Mom yelled for me to run, to save myself, but there was no way on God's earth I would leave her with those monsters. I exited the brush, showed myself, and walked toward Cruz.

"Leave her alone! It's me you want. She hasn't done a damn thing to any of you!"

Cruz chuckled, spoke into his walkie-talkie, and said he had both of us. Minutes later, Mateo, Elan, and the other man—the one who had been in the vehicle with Mateo the day before—approached us. I still didn't know his name.

"So, Mitch, you and your mama here are more inventive than I gave you credit for. How did you get those links stretched out enough to separate them from the chains?"

I shrugged. I wasn't about to tell him we used the spikes in case they put us back in the same spot again. He walked to me and stood a foot from my face.

"I asked you a question, Pig."

"I don't remember how we got out. We're starving, delirious, and everything is a blur."

"A blur? Let me show you what a blur actually is." With

a sudden thrust of his fist to my face, he knocked me to the ground. I felt like I'd been hit with a battering ram. My ears rang, and blood poured from my nose. His time behind bars had definitely made Mateo a much stronger man than I'd remembered.

Mom screamed profanities I'd never heard her utter. She was at her wit's end, and I was sure she would have a heart attack before long. Mateo backhanded her across the face, and I leapt from the ground just to be put back down. That time, I was kicked in the ribs too. I writhed back and forth, certain my ribs were cracked.

"Get up, Cannon. It's time to go. If you can't keep up, I'll kill your mom and then you. I'll leave you both out here for the panthers to eat. Now move!"

I stood, and everything began to spin. After grabbing a tree trunk, I was able to steady myself. Mateo gave me a shove, and we began walking, yet I had no idea where he was taking us. The only thing I knew for sure was that we were going in the opposite direction of that broken-down cocaine lab.

"Where are we going?" I knew that every word I spoke could lead to another beating, but I had to find out something. I might die that day, but at least if I did, I would do whatever I could first to find a way to get my mom out of the mess we were in.

"Shut up. Every time you speak, your mother is going to get slapped," Mateo said.

I couldn't see my mom to mouth how sorry I was and that I loved her—they made her walk behind me for just that reason. It was pure torture not to know how she was doing, whether she was falling or breathing too hard and if she needed a rest. I tripped with almost every step and was sure she did too. I tried to think of what day it was as we trudged through the brush.

We left Tampa on Friday, were at sea until Saturday morning, and then got kidnapped that day. We spent the night in the jungle, so is it Sunday? No, we spent two nights in the jungle. That means it's Monday. The ship has left Cozumel and is heading back to Tampa. I'm supposed to go to work on Wednesday, and Mom should be spending that day showing pictures and telling Meg and Marie all the wonderful things we did on our land excursions. Instead, we're plowing through a jungle with armed men whose intensions are still unknown. No matter what, in the end, I'm sure they'll kill us. If only—

My thoughts were interrupted by Mateo calling out instructions.

"Alejandro and Elan, get these two secured and put them in the middle seat. Cruz, you'll drive, and I'll sit in the back. If either of them try anything, they'll get a bullet to the back of the head."

I finally knew the anonymous man's name—Alejandro. If we ever got out of our predicament, I needed to remember as much as possible. I memorized the license plate and the type of vehicle we would be in. It was a black Suburban, not the same SUV as before. This one was bigger and had three rows of seats. We were zip-tied again and pushed into the middle row, me on the left and Mom on the right. I would be behind the driver, Cruz, just like last time, but we were on a different road. The one near the spot where we'd spent the night was behind us. At least I knew there was more than one road or long driveway that went into the jungle. If only I knew which direction we were facing. I glanced out the window to get a read on the time, but the sun was nearly straight up, which didn't tell me anything. I wondered what Royce and Rue were doing.

Are they concerned that I haven't communicated with them since Saturday morning, and what about Marie? Her worry radar has to be off the charts. She must have called the precinct to ask if I've been in touch, didn't she?

The men climbed into the vehicle, with Cruz behind the wheel, Alejandro riding shotgun, and Mateo and Elan in the back and ready to strike with any wrong move on our part. I watched for road signs and landmarks that could tell us where we were going, not that I knew anything about the area. If we ended up on the highway, I would at least know if we were going north or south because of the sea.

Cruz turned over the engine and backed up. He went in reverse for about a quarter mile then stopped and turned left onto another dirt road. My worst fears were realized. We were going deeper into the jungle, and I doubted that anyone looking for us would find us anytime soon.

Chapter 44

It took an hour of precious time before the officers were there with the man who had been Alejandro's driver. During that time, Royce, Rue, and the others had checked out the two locations in Playa—both dead ends.

Back at the Federales headquarters, they brainstormed how to get the driver to talk. Squealing on the drug cartels was dangerous and meant certain death if the person was found out.

The American police had no pull in Mexico, but the local FBI, the Federales, and the Playa del Carmen police did. There was always a sense of caution between the agencies, especially with the local police, who knew that somebody, even Roberto's own officers, could be on the take.

After delivering the man to Roberto and the others, the officers were asked to leave. At the end of the table, Royce and Rue sat quietly, each with paper and pen ready for taking notes.

"Do you know why you've been brought here?" Roberto asked after the young man sat down.

He stared straight ahead with his arms crossed as if in

indignation. "No, and I haven't done anything wrong."

"Nobody is accusing you of anything. We need answers to a few questions, and you're exactly the person who can give us those answers."

The young man grunted.

"Now, go ahead and state your name."

"You already know it, or you wouldn't have found me."

Pedro leaned forward. "We aren't playing games here, so do as the commander asks."

"Armando Castillo."

Royce paged through his notes as if looking for something. When he found it, he tapped Dave's shoulder and whispered in his ear, "We need a minute."

With a head tip, Dave asked for a short break. He and Royce needed to speak privately with Pedro. The men stepped out of the room and into the corridor.

Pedro looked puzzled. "What's going on? We just got started."

"How common is the last name Castillo?" Royce asked.

"Common enough. Why?"

"Coincidentally, it's also the last name of the tour company owner. Do you think they can actually be involved or possibly on Mateo's payroll? It could explain how Mateo knew Mitch had a tour booked."

"True, but it doesn't explain how they knew Mitch was in Mexico."

Royce groaned. "I know, but when Tom sends the text messages through, we might learn more. You need to press Armando about his job or who his family members are and what they do for a living. If his family owns that tour group, they might know exactly where Mitch and Mary are right now."

"Okay." Pedro pointed his chin at the door. "Let's go inside, and I'll ask those questions."

Once they were all in their seats, the questioning continued, that time with Pedro taking the reins.

"Armando, do you work?"

"Yeah, I haul people around."

Pedro raised his brows. "Explain that in detail, please."

"I give people lifts when they need a lift, then they pay me. End of story."

"Hmm … there must be more to it than that. How did you get into that line of work?"

"Let's just say it's a family enterprise."

"A family enterprise, you say? As in Castillo's Riviera Maya Private Tours?"

Armando broke eye contact and fidgeted.

"So, Alejandro Nunez is a client or a friend?"

Armando pulled back. "You following me?"

"He's a criminal and you're hauling him around, so of course we're following you." Pedro leaned in closer and with a deeper, more threatening voice continued. "Where did you take Alejandro?"

Armando shrugged. "When? I've picked him up a lot."

Pedro slapped the table, and Armando jumped. "The last time you picked him up. He hasn't been home since, and you know it. Don't play games with us, or you'll quickly see my bad side."

"Um… I don't remember. That was a few days back."

Pedro looked at Roberto and laughed. "You have some available cots in your jail, don't you?"

"Of course we do. We welcome guests like Armando to come and stay for a while."

Rue gave Royce a raised brow, jotted down a message, and passed it to Pedro, who read it silently then nodded.

The Federales and local police meant business, and a charge against the private tour company as coconspirators could ruin them financially. That angle had to be used against Armando to get answers.

"So, listen closely, Armando, because this is what's going to happen. We're quite certain that you know what's going on, who's calling the shots, where Alejandro went, and who was involved in kidnapping Detective Mitch Cannon and his mother. A black SUV was caught on video surveillance in the parking lot where the tour buses wait. We saw Mrs. Cannon and Mitch climb into it. There was a driver and a male passenger—both big men. I'd bet my last tortilla that the black SUV came from the Castillo's Riviera Maya Private Tours fleet. Am I right?" Pedro slapped the table again with a loud *smack*.

"I, um, I don't have any idea."

Roberto laughed. "Okay, we'll play it your way. You'll get locked up, and we'll shut down your family business on kidnapping charges. They'll never recover, they'll go broke and end up in jail, too, and you'll be considered a pariah to everyone who knows you." Roberto folded his hands. "Talk now or the entire family goes down."

"Okay, okay!" Armando covered his face with his hands and cried. "I wanted to feel like a big shot by driving those drug dealers around. They paid me well, my family turned a blind eye, and we had plenty of vehicles to use whenever they were needed."

"Where is Alejandro, and is he with Mateo Garcia? Who drove that black SUV, and who was the passenger? Tell us now!"

Armando wiped his tears away. "They'll kill me if I talk."

"And you'll die in prison if you don't." Roberto tapped his nails against the table then checked the time. "You have one minute to tell us everything, or I'll handcuff you myself."

"I don't know everything! I'm not one of them."

"You made yourself one of them by carrying out their illegal tasks. You supplied the kidnap vehicle for them. Now, where did you deliver that vehicle to?"

"The same place I dropped off Alejandro, but I swear I didn't know what they were going to do with it. They said they needed it for a few days, and then they returned it to the business and exchanged it for a larger SUV last night."

"Why?"

"I don't know! I swear!"

Pedro jerked his chin for Armando to continue.

"I dropped off Alejandro at a small casa where two women lived—one old and one young. I didn't ask who they were."

"Where was it?" Pedro asked.

"North of Tulum near the cenotes."

"Who was there besides the women?"

"Several men, one who Alejandro said was a big shot, but

he didn't tell me their names."

From his phone, Royce pulled up a picture of Mateo. He slid the phone across the table. "Was this man the big shot?"

Armando nodded.

"And you dropped off Alejandro there when?"

"Last Friday."

Pedro stood. "Take us there now."

Royce pointed with his chin. "Don't forget the laptop."

Chapter 45

We turned off on a half-dozen roads as we went deeper into remote areas. I hadn't seen a single house, barn, shed—or human being other than the ones in the vehicle with us.

Suddenly, Mom piped up. I tried to quiet her, but she wasn't having it. I feared Mateo would club her in the head too.

"Why do you hate my son so much? What has he done to any of you?"

Mateo laughed. "The old woman has guts. I'll give her that. Your son tried to play me for a fool by impersonating my friend Luis. Alejandro here went to Puerto Morelos on Saturday and watched as the Federales thought they were going to lure me into a store to pick up a new phone and money. That was your son's idea, Mary." Mateo huffed. "You really think we're stupid, don't you, Cannon?"

I knew better than to answer.

"By the way, Detective Pig, where is Luis?"

"In jail, where you'll be soon enough too." I knew that comment would get me a punch to the back of the head, and it did. I shook it off and glanced at Mom. Tears pooled in her eyes then dropped to her cheeks.

"One thing I do know, Cannon, is that you'll never have the pleasure of locking me up again."

I was seething and at the point that another blow to the head didn't matter. "Don't count on it, loser. Stranger things have happened."

Cruz drove for another twenty minutes, and during that time, I never saw the Caribbean. We were always on dirt roads under thick tree canopies, and for all I knew, he could be driving in circles just to throw us off. Everything looked the same no matter what road he turned on.

The Suburban finally slowed to a stop, and Cruz killed the engine then made a call. He spoke in Spanish, so I had no idea what he was saying. We sat there, but I didn't know why. The men spoke to each other, and even though I had no idea what they were saying, it was evident we were waiting for something.

Mom gave me a concerned look, and I prayed that she wouldn't say a word. Thankfully, she kept quiet. We were running out of strength and needed food and water. I had to ask for some, no matter the consequences. I turned slightly in the seat and looked at Mateo.

"Hey, what the hell do you think you're doing?"

"We need food. Neither of us has had a thing to eat since Saturday morning. Our water has run out too. Please, even if you don't give me anything, give my mom something to eat and drink. She's seventy years old and can't tolerate too much more of this. She'll die as an innocent woman who just wanted to enjoy a cruise for her seventieth birthday. She's done you no harm."

"She can wait like the rest of us."

"Wait for what?"

"Wait for whatever I say to wait for. Now shut up and turn around. Don't look at me again."

I did as told. I didn't want to push my luck, but as I looked at my mom, I saw her lips move as she silently prayed.

My ears perked when I heard what sounded like a vehicle coming up from behind. I had no idea why or whether that was a good or bad sign, but for Mom and me, it might not be a sign at all and just another plan Mateo had come up with.

When I heard a car door open and close, I wanted to look back, but I'd already been warned not to turn my head, so I stared at my lap.

"Okay, everyone out," Mateo ordered.

I wondered if that was it—if our lives were about to end with a shot to the head in the jungle.

"Get in the van."

I cautiously looked to our rear, and a van was parked behind us. A man I'd never seen before waved us to the side door.

"Get in and sit down in the middle seats."

We did as instructed, then Mateo and Elan climbed in the back behind us. Elan held a gun in plain sight, probably as a warning so I wouldn't try anything. Alejandro and Cruz got in the front, Cruz behind the wheel. He backed up.

Next to Elan sat a cooler. He wiggled his finger at Mom and told her to come in the back.

I stopped her as she protested. "Mom, go ahead. You'll be

fine." I watched as she climbed into the rear seat and sat between the two men as instructed. Mateo pulled a knife from the sheath on his belt.

"Turn around, old lady, so I can cut your restraints. You can thank your son for this. Personally, I don't care if you die."

Mom followed his instructions, and her body shook as he sliced her zip ties. She rubbed her wrists and waited with her eyes focused on me.

I watched Mateo's every move and saw him give Elan a subtle nod. Elan opened the cooler, pulled out a bottle of water and a sandwich, and gave them to Mom. I nearly cried with gratitude to the man that I hated more than anyone else.

Mom was torn. I could see it in her eyes. She cracked open the water bottle and leaned over the back of my seat but not before Elan reached out and grabbed her arm.

Mateo spoke up. "Let her share. It'll make me feel better about killing both of them. She can give him some of the sandwich too. Meanwhile, I need to send off a text to your boss, Sergeant Royce." He grinned at me. "Give me his number, and it better be right, or you'll be watching me end your mother's life."

At that moment, the only thing on my mind was restoring my energy with food so I could kill Mateo before he killed us.

Chapter 46

According to Armando, they were halfway to the home where he'd dropped off Alejandro. Four of them were in the car besides Armando—Royce, Rue, Dave, and Pedro. Roberto didn't have any jurisdiction outside Playa del Carmen, so he stayed there.

Royce and Rue sat in the back seat with Pedro while Dave drove and Armando called out directions.

"Check your email, Pedro."

Pedro opened his laptop and said the Wi-Fi was too weak while driving, but the fast-food restaurant directly ahead on the right could give him the signal he needed. The stop would only take a minute.

Dave pulled in and parked. "How's that?"

"It's good. The Wi-Fi is working." Pedro logged in and found the email that had come in just a few minutes earlier. "It's here, but it doesn't sound good. The subject line says, 'Uh-oh.'"

Royce frowned.

"You know the timeline, Sergeant Royce. Go ahead and check it yourself." Pedro passed the laptop to Royce, who scrolled through the dates.

"Let's begin on Thursday and see what Mitch and Mateo talked about when Mateo still thought he was communicating with Luis. There's got to be something that caused Tom to write that in the subject line." Royce began reading the texts. Nothing set off an alarm until he got to the texts that told Mateo a new phone with unlimited minutes and data, along with money, would ship to a drop spot in Puerto Morelos on Saturday. "What the hell is this?"

Rue looked from Royce to the screen. "What did you find?"

"The reason Tom wrote uh-oh. It looks like Mitch sent the next text to Mateo but it was meant for me. It says Mateo would be in Puerto Morelos on Saturday and I should find a drop spot there, along with the name of the ship Mitch and Mary were on and Mitch's stateroom number. Son of a bitch! It was Mitch himself who accidentally gave Mateo the heads-up."

"So that's why Mateo never showed at the drop spot, and instead, he and his boys were in Playa, waiting for Mitch and Mary to go on that private tour to the Mayan ruins. Everything was handed to Mateo on a silver platter, and they were ready and waiting for it."

"Exactly." Royce swirled his finger above his head. "Let's continue on. Armando, you're going to tell us when we're a few blocks out. We're not taking any chances since that house could be full of Mateo's men. There's no way we're going to let them make a move on us, especially if Mitch and Mary are among them. Got it?"

"Yes, I've got it."

Ten minutes later, Armando held up his hand. "You should slow down now. That casa is just around the next curve on the right."

"Were any vehicles there when you dropped off Alejandro?"

"Yes, a white truck and two black SUVs from our fleet."

"Two?"

"Yes. Like I said, several men were there. Nobody has vehicles of their own. It would be too easy for them to be tracked."

"Who owns the white truck?"

Armando said he didn't know but possibly the women.

"Pull over and park, Dave. We're going to spread out and go in quietly." Royce jerked his head toward the back of the car. "Get in the trunk, kid, and if you make a peep, I'll come back and silence you. Understand?"

Armando nodded, and when the trunk was opened, he climbed in.

"Give me your cell phone. You'll get it back later."

Saying something in Spanish, Armando handed it over. Royce cuffed his hands behind his back in case he tried to get out, then he slammed the trunk lid.

The four men cautiously walked along the edge of the road until they reached the curve. There, they spread out through the tree cover and moved in until they were within fifty feet of the house.

Royce raised his hand, and everyone stopped. The rear door opened, and the old woman walked out carrying a basket. She began hanging wet clothes on a line stretched between the trees.

With a hand signal to the others, Pedro moved in alone and approached the woman while the others kept their eyes on the glassless windows. A hand wave told them it was okay to move in.

Pedro and Dave did the talking while Royce and Rue watched their surroundings. Seconds later, the younger woman walked out.

From what the old woman had passed on, Elan Sanchez was her nephew, the other men were his friends, and she was paid three thousand pesos to feed and shelter the men for two days and nights. They left Saturday morning, one man for Puerto Morelos and the others for Playa del Carmen. Dave asked if they'd been back or if the women knew where any of them lived. She'd told them that Elan lived alone near the jungle sanctuary, but they knew nothing about the others.

"So that's it?" Rue asked as he stared at a scrawny dog lying in the dirt. "None of that helps us find out where they are now."

Pedro took over and asked if the women had heard the men talking about a man named Mitch Cannon.

The young woman looked nervous, but Pedro pressed on. She finally admitted that she'd heard Mitch's name mentioned and that Mateo Garcia said he was going to kill both Mitch and his mother. The men thanked the women and returned to the car.

"Where the hell is the jungle sanctuary?" Rue asked.

"Inland from the cenotes," Pedro said, "and near where the drug busts took place years back. In the jungle, they built cocaine labs that we had been monitoring for months until the time was right. We moved in, destroyed everything, and took a dozen men into custody."

"Can you remember how to get to those labs?"

"Yes, that's something I'll never forget."

"Good. Let's check out those spots first and then find Elan's home. My guess is that they're off the grid somewhere just like the old woman's house was, or they've moved farther away."

"Meaning they've already killed Mitch and Mary?" Rue asked.

Royce wrinkled his forehead. "I doubt that Mateo would kill him without getting something in return. Mitch's life is too valuable to waste."

Dave popped the trunk. "What do you want to do with this guy?"

"Let him out. He can use his cell phone to call for a pickup from here." Royce uncuffed Armando, handed the phone back to him, and told him to stay out of trouble.

Pedro chimed in. "If we find out you're driving drug dealers and murderers around, you and your familia will end up in prison alongside them. Understand?"

"Yes, sir."

"Good, because we'll be watching your family's business closely." Pedro got in behind the wheel. "I'll drive since I know the way."

Chapter 47

"What's this?"

"What?"

Royce looked over his shoulder at Devon. "I missed a text. It must have come in while we were creeping through the woods." Royce tapped the screen and began reading. "I don't believe this shit. It's from Mateo, and he says he wants five million dollars ransom for Mitch and Mary's safe return. Once the money is wired to his account, he'll have someone drop off both of them to the Federales office in Playa. If not, they'll die, and their bodies will never be found. He wants the money by three o'clock today. That's impossible to do!"

"How the hell would he even have your phone number?" Devon asked.

"Mitch must have given it to him, but I doubt that he did it willingly."

"And that tells us Mitch and Mary are still alive." Rue looked out the window. "If only there were more cell towers around here and technical people available to triangulate their location."

Pedro groaned. "Back in these dense areas, you're considered lucky to get cell reception at all." He turned onto a narrow dirt road. "It isn't far now, only ten minutes, and then a walk through the jungle to reach the broken-down lab."

"How far of a walk?" Royce asked.

Pedro shrugged. "Fifteen minutes or so. Keep your elbows in the car. The road gets even more narrow the farther we go in."

"Does this road actually go somewhere?" Rue asked.

"Only to the cocaine lab. The drug lord's minions carved out this path with machetes years back. I'm actually surprised we can get through here, so that has to mean—"

Royce sat up straight. "That somebody else has been back here too."

"Exactly." Pedro slowed to a stop a few minutes later. "We're here, and we're alone."

"How do you know?"

"Because there aren't any vehicles back here. This path is the only road in. Someone could walk through the jungle from other directions, but finding where the lab once stood would be difficult." He looked at the ground then tipped his head at the others. "Tire tracks going in and out, and they still look relatively fresh."

Rue fumbled with his phone. "Damn, it's hard to see back here."

"Yeah, the sun doesn't filter through these trees unless it's straight above the canopy. It'll be better in about a half hour."

Royce walked to Rue's side. "What are you trying to do anyway?"

"Get a few pics of the possible crime scene. I've got another idea too."

Dave scratched his head. "Yeah, what's that?"

"We couldn't get through on Mitch's phone. My question is, was it actually turned off, or was the reception too bad to get a call through?"

Royce raised a brow. "Hard to say. It just went to voicemail."

"I'll try it now." On his phone, Rue tapped Mitch's name and waited then shook his head. "Still goes to voicemail, so I guess it is turned off. I'll try Mary's."

"Mary's?"

"Sure. Why not? Maybe hers is still on."

"Why would it be?" Dave asked.

"Gotta try everything, don't we?" Rue tapped the number for Mary that Marie had given him the day before. They waited.

Royce jerked his head toward the jungle. "Come on. Let's check out where they made the cocaine."

Dave pointed at the ground. "Unless this is an animal trail, I'd say people have been traipsing back and forth through here."

"Everyone stop! I hear something." Devon headed to the brush where the sound came from. It went from ringing to Mary's greeting when the call went to voicemail. He frantically ripped through the bushes and pulled up a purse. "I found it. This has to belong to Mary." Devon looked inside and found a wallet, devoid of money, and a phone. "It's hers. The ID belongs to Mary Cannon, and this is her phone. They were definitely here and possibly still are."

Following Pedro, the men rushed down the matted path,

over logs, and through tangly vines until they reached what was left of the platform.

"This is it," Pedro said.

Everyone did a three-sixty.

"I don't see shit other than a rotting platform on the jungle floor," Dave said.

Pedro swatted his neck. The annoying mosquito that had just bitten him quickly turned into a mashed bug and blood. "Yeah, it doesn't take long for the environment to reclaim itself. Let's look around. There's got to be evidence of someone being back here."

The men walked around the platform, and Rue caught sight of a chain lying among the vines. He followed it to a tree several feet away.

"Got something. Looks like Mitch and Mary may have been chained here at some point. The chain is too new to be from the cocaine era."

Everyone went to Rue's spot.

"That's definitely new. Look around for another one. Either they were together here, or they were separated. For Mary's sake, I hope they were together," Pedro said.

"Got it! I found another chain on this side of the platform," Dave said. "The question is, why move them, and where did they go?"

Royce pulled out his phone while Rue snapped pictures. "I don't know what Mateo is thinking, but I need to contact the precinct and tell them about the ransom demand." Royce tried several times, but the call kept dropping. "We need to get out of these trees and back to the path. I should be able to get a signal from there."

Back at the vehicle, Royce tried one more time. If the call didn't go through, he would have to wait until they got on the main road to make another attempt. Everyone watched as he dialed the Habersham precinct.

He nodded. "It's ringing in Bleu's office." After three rings, a familiar and welcome voice answered. "Bleu, it's Royce. No, we haven't found them yet, but Mateo just contacted me with a ransom demand for five million dollars for Mitch and Mary's safe return. Yeah, I know it's unlikely that they'll let them go. He wants the money wired to his account by three p.m. He says he'll kill Mitch and Mary otherwise. Uh-huh. Do what? Someone picked up the package on Sunday? Hell yeah, tell Tech to start tracking that phone immediately. We had no idea that the package was picked up. Yes, call me back the second Tom knows something." Royce clicked off the call. "I don't believe this shit. Somebody walked into El Rancho in Puerto Morelos yesterday and claimed the package. If that person turned on the phone, Tech can track it."

Rue fist pumped the air. "It's about damn time we caught a break."

Royce snickered. "And with any luck, we'll catch Mateo Garcia too."

Chapter 48

The van turned right into a short dirt driveway then pulled around behind the house. The men got out and headed to the door. Just then, the young woman came out, waving and yelling frantically. In Spanish, she told the men that the Federales had been there and had asked about Mitch Cannon. Mateo and the others had to leave. She and her mother couldn't risk being mixed up in their illegal activities.

"Damn it!" Mateo yelled out. "Alejandro, get over here. What do you know about your driver? Is he trustworthy?"

"Yes, he's always been."

"Then how did the Federales know that we've been to this house?"

"I have no idea, Mateo. Shall I call Armando?"

"No, and I don't want you to have any contact with him again."

"Then how do we get the vehicles if we cut ties with them?"

"Find another company if you have to. He had to be the leak. He dropped you off here and saw the rest of us. There's nobody else it could be." Mateo raised a brow at each man. "Or is there?"

"No, sir," they said at the same time.

"Good, then get in the van and put Mary back in the middle seat. We have to find another place to hunker down. We can't go to Elan's house. He's the old woman's nephew, and he's probably been compromised." Mateo turned to the young woman and asked if the Federales were told that Elan was the old woman's nephew. She nodded.

"It's too risky to stay here since the Federales might come back." Mateo climbed into the rear seat and ordered Cruz to go. "I'll think of a place to stay while you drive."

Chapter 49

"Go to the Riviera Maya tour company location," Royce said. "We need to know every vehicle Armando has used to drive Alejandro around in and where they went. Somebody picked up that phone and money, and I doubt that Mateo would be reckless enough to step foot in Puerto Morelos. He knows that the Federales have been watching the area for him, plus he's kind of preoccupied with Mitch right now."

"Good point," Dave said. "Pedro, do you know where they're located?"

"I do. They're twenty minutes south of Playa."

Pedro backed down the dirt road until he could turn around. They reached the tour company at noon and, once inside, asked to speak to the owner or manager.

Several minutes later, a stocky man with graying hair came from a back room. "I'm Miguel Castillo, the owner. How can I help you gentlemen?"

Rue caught sight of Armando. "Actually, sir, we need to speak to Armando first if you don't mind."

"Armando? You know my son?"

"Yes. He's a regular driver, right?"

"He is." Miguel called out and waved Armando over. "These men want to speak to you, but don't be long. You have to pick up Mr. Delgado at the harbor in a half hour." Miguel stepped over to the reception counter and began talking to the woman behind it.

A worried expression covered Armando's face, then he whispered to the group. "What are you doing here? My father doesn't know Mateo Garcia kidnapped a US detective. Please—"

"If you want discretion, then you better speak up now," Royce said, "or I'll call your padre over."

"Okay, okay. I thought I answered all your questions before." Armando glanced at his father then tipped his head toward the other side of the room. "Let's go over there. I don't want him to hear our conversation. So, what do you want now?"

Pedro took over. "We know somebody went to Puerto Morelos yesterday and picked up a package from a store. Who was it, and did you drive them there?"

"Um…"

"Speak up, kid, or daddy is going to learn everything. We'll arrest your entire family and shut down this operation right now," Royce said.

With slumped shoulders, Armando admitted that he'd picked up Alejandro on Sunday and taken him to Puerto Morelos. "He went into the store and, minutes later, came back with a box. He tore it open and found a phone and five hundred dollars inside. He gave me a hundred-dollar bill for the ride and said to keep the pickup to myself."

"Did he activate the phone?" Royce asked.

"Not while I was with him, but he did say he was going to use it for himself. Something about his old phone being a dinosaur."

"And what about that larger vehicle you said they swapped the other one for last night?" Rue asked. "Can you track it?"

"We can't. Invasion of privacy act. The only time the tracking device is activated is if the vehicle isn't returned when agreed upon. I can't activate anything without that vehicle's code, and my father handles all of that. He'd want to know why I'm asking about it."

"Hold on." Royce made a call to Savannah. He needed to speak with Tom in Tech. The phone rang twice, then Tom picked up.

"Tech, Tom Branch speaking."

"Tom, it's Royce. Can you see if that burner phone has been activated, and if it has, can you track it?"

"Yeah, sure. It's going to take a few minutes, though. Can I call you back?"

"Okay, but make it as soon as humanly possible."

"Got it."

Royce hung up and wagged his finger at Armando. "If we need to come back here, it isn't going to look good for you. This is my card." He discreetly handed his contact card to Armando. "Anything that Mateo and his boys want from you better run through me first. Understand?"

"Yes, sir."

"Good. Now make up a story for your father about why

we were here, and like I said, if we need to come back, that means your family business is going down."

The men left, grabbed lunch at a cantina in Chacalal, and waited for Tom's call.

Chapter 50

I watched out the window in silence. Mom's head bobbed forward. She was dozing off, and that was good. She needed to rest.

"Cruz, turn right on Highway 10. I know the perfect spot where we'll wait to hear back about the ransom money." Mateo patted Mitch's shoulder and chuckled. "You're really going to fall for this place."

Cruz drove northwest out of Tulum, past the sites and restaurants. Where we were going, I didn't know, but my head spun when I heard Mateo mention the ransom money. He had actually sent the text to Royce, so it wasn't just a scare tactic on his part. That meant our lives depended on whether the money was sent, and I already knew what the outcome would be.

I paid close attention to the route, trying to memorize every town we passed and every turn we made. The sites would be crucial to remember if we had another chance to escape.

Fifteen minutes later, after Mateo and his men spoke back and forth in Spanish, Cruz made a right-hand turn down a paved one-lane road. There was no street sign with a name on it for me to remember.

Mateo leaned forward between Mom and me, and his movement startled her awake.

"Once we get to the spot, we're going to go for a little walk. You two will be impressed when you see where we end up. Not many people know about this particular anomaly of nature. It's quite amazing." Mateo spoke again in Spanish, and Cruz nodded. They all laughed, which unnerved me.

Mom looked into my eyes, and I saw fear and sadness in hers. She was expecting the end to be near, and so was I. There had to be something I could do other than accept our fate. Royce wouldn't be able to get the ransom money together, and I knew the FBI would refuse to pay terrorists and kidnappers like Mateo. We were on our own, and although I didn't know the time frame Mateo had given Royce, nobody would find us before it was too late anyway. Mom and I would die without our family at our sides. At least we'd be together, though—I hoped—but our bodies would never be returned to the United States because they would never be found.

"A left turn is coming up and then a right fifty yards after that. We'll be at our location in ten minutes." Mateo taunted me with his sick humor. "So what do you think, Pig? Will your sergeant come through with five million bucks in time, or will he let you fry like bacon?" Mateo elbowed me in the ear as he laughed. "Get it? Pig and bacon? Maybe I should say you'll be swimming with the fish instead. I wonder if people can swim with their hands bound behind their backs."

"I wouldn't know. Why don't you try it on yourself?" His reaction to that comment nearly broke my jaw, and Mom began to cry again.

"Shut up, Cannon, and shut up that old hag, or she'll go first."

I rearranged myself and went quiet. That was when I felt the burr on the seat belt assembly jammed behind me. There was a chance I could use that to my advantage if I could weaken or cut through my zip ties. I would have to position my wrists in the right spot and saw back and forth without my actions being noticed, but if we were close to the end location, I wouldn't have much time to get it done.

Why didn't I know that burr was there before? I could have cut through the zip ties by now.

I sawed back and forth for the next ten minutes, still trying to maintain a minimal amount of movement. Mom glanced my way—she probably felt the vibration on the seat—but when I frowned, she turned her attention out the window, perhaps so Mateo wouldn't suspect anything. I thought about the best way to go forward—cut the tie completely, which would be noticed immediately when I exited the van, or leave enough held together so I could spring on one of the men, grab a gun, and shoot our way out of the predicament I had gotten us into.

Yeah, right. Like I'm some kind of superhero.

No matter what, I had to keep in mind that Mom was still secured with the zip ties and couldn't run nearly as fast as I could.

I felt the zip tie give. It was time to stop sawing. I was sure that I could snap them at the right time. First, I would have to weigh the situation—know where everyone was, who had a gun in their possession, and who would be the easiest to overpower.

After we'd made the last turn, Mateo pointed at a spot to park. "This is it. Stop the van."

Cruz did as instructed, and we remained seated and waited for Mateo's next order. He pulled out his cell phone and frowned.

"Humph. Your boss mustn't care about you or the old lady. I haven't gotten a response from him at all."

"Maybe your message didn't go through, so why don't you send it again?" I needed time, and I would say or do anything to have more of it. I had to come up with a plan, and it had to be something that would work, or Mom and I would both die at Mateo's hand.

"Yeah, it can't hurt." Mateo tapped his phone's keys. "Damn it, my battery is almost dead. It's not doing anything. Alejandro, let me use your phone."

Alejandro passed his phone to Mateo.

"Get a new phone?"

"Um, yeah, from my brother for my birthday."

"Nice. Okay, Cannon, what's Royce's number again?"

I rattled it off, and he tapped the keys then sent the message for the second time.

"I'll hang on to your phone for now, Alejandro. I want to see if the pig's boss responds." Mateo grabbed the handle and slid the side door open. "Get out, both of you."

Mom climbed out, and I followed, making sure that the

zip ties were covered with my hands.

"Move aside. I'll lead," Mateo said.

I glanced at each man to see who was armed and who wasn't. Elan and Cruz, both the largest men, had guns exposed on their hips. I didn't see anything on Alejandro or Mateo right then, but that didn't mean much since Mateo had held a gun on us earlier.

Mateo led the way down a narrow path. Cruz walked behind him, and Elan and Alejandro took up the rear. We walked for a good distance, which gave me time to formulate a plan. No matter what I did, it would be dangerous for Mom and me. That much I knew. I said a silent prayer for guidance and was sure the man upstairs knew I needed help.

Chapter 51

"I'm putting you on Speaker, Tom, so the others can listen in. What have you got?"

"Sergeant Bleu is here with me, and I'll put you on Speaker as well. Okay, the burner phone is active, and I'm tracking it as we speak."

"Great. We just left Chacalal. Hang on one sec. I have a text coming in." Royce took a look and saw that he'd gotten a second text from Mateo, one even more threatening. Mateo must have used a different phone since his previous text wasn't showing up. It was urgent that they track down Mitch right away. "Okay, I'm back, guys. That was another text from Mateo, and he's getting madder by the minute because I didn't respond to his earlier text. We need to find Mitch now!"

"Raleigh, it's Bleu. Tom is pulling up a map of the area. It looks like you need to continue to Tulum and then go northwest on Highway 10. The tracking device shows that they turned right at Francisco Uh May, then left, and then another right shortly after that. For the last few minutes, the phone has been moving slower."

"Like they're driving slow or walking?"

"Can't tell, but they're probably a half hour ahead of you. Anything can happen in thirty minutes, so you need to pick up the pace."

"Got it. I have to stall Mateo with a bs text. I'll call you back in ten minutes." Royce ended the call and had to think. "I need to send Mateo a response that'll buy us time and keep him calm. Help me out, guys."

Because Dave was an FBI agent and the only other American besides Royce and Rue, he knew how the US handled kidnapping demands. He was sure that Mateo wasn't well-educated in American legalities, how long it took to get that amount of money together, or what department was in charge of wiring ransom money to a bank in another country.

"I can buy us some extra time. Hand me your phone, Raleigh." Dave tipped his wrist—it was pushing one o'clock. He tapped away at the phone keys and told Mateo that, because of the chain of command he needed to go through to authorize a money transfer like that, and the amount of money the demand was for, it would be at least four more hours before Mateo would see any of the money in his account. They would need until five o'clock before the transfer was completed. Nobody had that kind of money in personal accounts, and moving large sums like that out of police department funds involved a lot of red tape.

"There. I sent it, and he's going to be pissed, but what are his options? We'll demand proof of life every half hour, or he'll never see a penny of that money. Of course, we know he'll never see a cent anyway, but at least that'll keep him preoccupied while we surround him and his thugs. We're going to rescue Mitch and Mary before Mateo even knows what happened." Dave handed the phone back to Royce and looked over at Pedro. "What we need from you, Pedro, is more Federales to meet us at Highway 10 and accompany us to the location where Mateo took Mitch and Mary."

"Not a problem. I'll arrange it right now." Pedro tapped his earbud, made the call, and told his men to bring ropes in case they were needed. They were heading into cenote territory. He hung up and continued driving. "We're good to go. Another ten Federales will meet us at the highway entrance."

Royce sucked in a deep gulp of air and let it out slowly. "Now, as long as Mateo stays put, we'll sneak in, surround them, and take them by surprise. We'll haul that son of a bitch back to the US, where he'll sit on death row until he's executed, and that's exactly where he belongs."

Royce called the tech department back, and Bleu told him that the phone was still moving at a very slow speed.

"Raleigh, Tom and I looked at a satellite view of the area they're in. It's remote and riddled with cenotes. Not the kind that are open to the public either with safety railings and so forth. There isn't a building, a parking lot, or anything else that screams that another human being knows of that place."

"Is the phone moving in the direction of the cenotes?"

"I'm afraid so," Bleu said.

"Shit. What's the topography like? Is there cover where we can surround them and take them by surprise?"

"Yes, same as most of that area—trees and brush to hide behind."

"Okay, we're turning onto Highway 10 now. Pedro, the head of the Federales in this area, has called in more officers to lend a hand. As soon as we reach Francisco Uh May, I'll call you back."

"Roger that."

Chapter 52

Alejandro was my size, and Elan had three inches and thirty pounds on me. Elan was also armed. I still didn't have a plan, but I slowed my pace to put some distance between Mateo and Cruz and the rest of us. I said my mother was struggling with the walk and asked if we could slow down a little. They seemed to buy my story and continued with whatever they were discussing and laughing about in Spanish. That worried me. For all I knew, they could be laughing about our upcoming fate.

I knew Mateo was counting on that ransom money, and I was sure that just before he put a bullet in my head, he would thank me for the five million dollars to fund his Mexican drug empire.

Mom gave me another glance, which I met with my own. I had to warn her that I was about to make a move, but I couldn't do it verbally. Whatever I did had to be a surprise to everyone, including her. If we lived through it, I would apologize later.

I needed tree cover not only for myself but also for Mom. Lying across the path ahead of us was a large log. I would use it to my advantage since it was all I had. I watched as Mateo and Cruz climbed over it and continued on. It was now or never.

I had to move with lightning speed for my surprise attack to work. Either I would be shot and killed, or Elan and Alejandro would. With a final look at where Mom would land, I snapped my zip ties, then I pushed her deep into the bushes. I spun and punched Elan in the face as hard as I could since he was the immediate threat. As he stumbled into Alejandro, I grabbed the gun from his holster then shot them both. I yelled for Mom to run, then I jumped into the bushes, where I would have some cover.

I still had Mateo and Cruz to deal with, and they were serious threats. I heard them yelling in Spanish—a disadvantage for me. I had no idea what their plan of attack was. Mom was in the distance, and I motioned for her to lie down and stay quiet. She nodded that she understood. A twig snapped to my left, but I couldn't see anyone. I crept forward and tried to remain invisible. Since Cruz was armed and Mateo had a knife, I needed to be as small of a target as possible. Staying behind trees, I would try to get a bead on Cruz since he was the biggest threat. His white shirt would be easy to see, and if I got off a decent shot, the blood on it would be noticeable too.

A flash of color came from thirty feet ahead of me, and something passed by. It had to be Mateo since I didn't see anything white. I fired and heard a grunt—it could have been a real hit or a ploy for me to come closer and investigate. I remained where I was and slowly turned my head to see if

Mom was still well-hidden. I couldn't see her anywhere, so I assumed she was good. Hoping to see more movement ahead of me, I stayed put, yet somebody had to make a move. The standoff had to end, and I needed to make sure Mom was okay. I looked at the ground and remembered the rock Mom had found when we were chained at the platform. I could throw one and startle Mateo or Cruz enough so they would move and I could get off a shot. It was an old tactic, but in the moment of high adrenaline and nerves on edge, people didn't think clearly. They would always turn to see where the noise came from.

A rock about the size of my fist was just two feet away. I would have to reach for it and hope I didn't make a sound, but it was all I had to use.

Cruz called out that he was going to find me and shoot me and my mother too. In those perfect few seconds when he was yelling, I grabbed the rock, pulled it from the earth, and threw it in the direction of his voice. That was when I saw white. Cruz moved just enough for me to get him in my sights. He gripped his gun as if ready to fire and stood against a tree to take aim, then I pulled the trigger. His scream was authentic, and I knew I'd hit my mark. His firing hand was useless, and his gun flew into the bushes. Mateo was still out there, and whether he was armed with a pistol or not, I didn't know, but right then, I had to secure Cruz's gun before he got to it. If push came to shove, he would shoot with his left hand since it was a matter of life and death.

I rushed him and knocked him to the ground. Even injured, he was still a strong man who could throw a punch.

I needed to avoid that at all costs. I jumped back and shot again, splintered his leg, and knew he couldn't go anywhere. I rifled through the bushes and felt the cold steel of his gun, jammed it into my waistband, then got sucker punched in the face when I stood. Mateo was only two feet away, and if he'd had a gun of his own, I would already be dead.

He bolted, and I gave chase. I would catch that killer and take him into custody or, if I had no other choice, shoot him dead where he stood. As Mateo zigged and zagged through the thick tree cover, I lost sight of him. Then by a stroke of luck, I caught a glimpse as he ran into a clearing about fifty feet ahead. I yelled out, "Mateo, stop, or I'll shoot you!"

He continued on. I fired a shot and missed, then he disappeared again behind what looked like jagged limestone formations.

"Damn it." Without eyes on him, I moved ahead cautiously. I reached the rocks, my gun drawn and ready as I peeked around the craggy edge that blocked my view. Just then, he yelled and pushed me from behind, and I lost my balance. I was free-falling but not before I had time to grab his pant leg and pull him with me. Seconds later, we plunged into ice-cold water. The guns were gone, likely sinking to the bottom of the cenote he'd pushed me into. Mateo had the upper hand. He knew what to expect, and he wasn't food deprived or exhausted either. He punched me and held me under water until I thought my lungs would burst. I folded my legs then with all my might kicked him in the gut as hard as I could. Mateo slammed into the stone edge behind him, knocked senseless for a few seconds. The sight I saw next threw me for a loop but was a godsend since my strength was dwindling fast.

Five Federales leapt into the cenote, helped me to the edge, and with ropes, pulled me out. I lay on the ground, coughing up water and trying to catch my breath. Then I saw them, the best sights any cop could ever hope to see—my boss, Raleigh Royce, and my best friend and partner, Devon Rue. I laughed and cried and begged them to find my mom.

"Don't worry, partner. We've already found her, and she's fine." Devon moved aside, and there stood my mom with tears running down her cheeks. She knelt next to me, and I'd never felt so much love come from one small but fierce seventy-year-old woman. She kissed my face and wept.

Chapter 53

After I'd caught my breath and was able to stand, I walked to the edge of the cenote and looked down into the thirty-foot hole. Mateo, in the middle and treading water, begged to be pulled up.

"Let that dog paddle for a while. He needs to feel helpless and exhausted just like we did." I turned to Royce. "Want to make the introductions?"

"You bet, Mitch. This here is Dave Camden, head of the FBI team from Mexico City, and to Dave's left is Pedro Torres, the commander of the local Federales in this area. The men who rescued you are from Pedro's team."

I shook hands and gave everyone hugs of gratitude. "You have no idea what having you here means to me and my mom." I put my arm around her, apologized for tossing her into the bushes, then finally smiled. We were safe. "What about the others?"

"Those two men fifty yards back are dead, and the big guy in the white shirt has two bullet holes in him, but he'll make it."

"That's too bad." I jerked my head toward the cenote.

"Go ahead and pull him up. I think I have about five minutes of strength left in me, if you know what I mean."

"You got it, Detective Cannon." Pedro spun his finger above his head and told his men to pull Mateo out.

After ten minutes of flailing while they tried to get the rope around him so he could climb the rock wall, Mateo was finally on dry ground.

"Can I have my five minutes with him now?"

"You bet." Pedro and his men headed to the cars with Dave and my mom. Rue and Royce stayed with me.

"You don't have to watch if you don't want to, but as long as I'm still on Mexican soil and there aren't any Mexican authorities to see my actions, I'm going to take full advantage of it."

Rue and Royce shrugged but didn't budge.

I walked up to Mateo, who was still lying on the ground. I kicked him in the ribs and punched him until my knuckles bled. "Hey, asshole. Remember when you said I'd never have the pleasure of locking you up again? Well, don't count on it, because I'll make sure it's me who slams that jail door where you'll sit until you go to GDCP."

He coughed. "Where?"

I snarled. "It's where you'll die by lethal injection." I knelt at his side, and with my fist cocked, I delivered a final blow to his jaw. "That one was for my mom."

He was knocked out cold. I walked ahead of Rue and Royce as they dragged him back to the vehicles. Pedro said they would throw him in their jail cell in Playa until we were ready to leave with him and return to the USA.

"It'll take a few days to process the paperwork," Pedro said as he looked me up and down, "but I think you and your mother need some rest anyway."

Royce spoke up. "Rue and I will take care of everything. Mary and Mitch need food, water, and plenty of R and R."

I watched as the Federales threw Mateo into the back of a cruiser. Cruz was seated in another one, headed to a hospital where they could tend to his injuries before he was thrown in jail. The bodies of Elan and Alejandro were placed in the back of the van we'd arrived in, and the Federales drove away with them.

Pedro left with his men, and Dave, Devon, Royce, Mom, and I headed to the Mayan Paradise, the hotel where everyone was staying.

Royce dialed the hotel from the car. "Hello, this is Sergeant Royce from Room 408. We're going to need a double suite near us on the fourth floor for the next couple of days. Yes, adjoining rooms 410 and 412 are perfect. Thanks." Royce hung up, looked over his shoulder at Mom and me sitting next to Devon, and smiled. "We're all set, buddy. You two can clean up. We'll order plenty of food to be delivered to your room, and when you're ready, you can tell us about your two-day nightmare."

I nodded, closed my eyes, and squeezed my mom's hand.

An hour later, we were in a beach hotel in Playa del Carmen. Everything that had taken place once we got off the ship seemed like a bad nightmare, and it was—a real one that had actually happened.

"Go ahead and get cleaned up, eat something, and then

relax," Rue said as he and Royce walked Mom and me to our rooms. "I'm in 406, and Sarge is in 408. Just call when you feel like talking."

I gave Devon a hug and thanked them both, then Mom and I stepped into my room.

"Mom, I'm going to shower and then—"

She gave me a tired grin. "We don't have any clean clothes."

"Crap, you're right. How about if Devon and Royce do a little shopping for us? Meanwhile, I'll have our clothes washed. We can lounge around in our bathrobes after our showers." I opened the door to her adjoining room and looked inside. It was nice. "Go ahead, Mom, and take as long as you need. I'll call the laundry service and tell them to pick up our clothes in an hour."

"You bet, honey. Mitch?"

"Yep?"

"I'm so proud of you. You're my favorite son."

I laughed and hugged her tightly. "And you're my favorite mom."

I made the call to the laundry department, got that squared away, then called Rue. "I need a favor, buddy."

"Name it."

"Mom and I don't have any clean clothes to put on."

"Yeah, you have a point. What do you need?"

"Just a change of clothes for each of us. The hotel's laundry service will pick up our dirty ones and wash them."

"Not a problem. You think my size will fit you?"

"Yeah, that'll be fine. Mom wears a size eight. Just grab

her a loose-fitting dress. Something tropical, colorful, and comfortable-looking."

"You got it. I'll have Royce go with me."

"Thanks, partner. I'm sure thankful for both of you."

"No sweat. I'll buzz your room in an hour."

Chapter 54

I'd never appreciated a shower more than I did that day and used nearly an entire bar of soap. What had seemed like inconsequential things before now seemed important. Our horrible experience opened my eyes to seize the day—carpe diem, as they said—and not take anything for granted. I realized during our trip how much of a warrior my mom was. Seventy years old meant nothing. She was strong, loving, and fierce, and I planned to remember that for the rest of my life. Going forward, I would do whatever I could to live up to her expectations and show her how much she meant to me.

I dried off, put on the guest bathrobe, and looked at my reflection after wiping the steam off the mirror.

"Wow."

Mateo had done a number on me, but by tomorrow, he would probably look as bad as I did. I brushed my teeth with the complimentary toothbrush and toothpaste then walked out to my balcony and took a seat. The sun had begun to set, and the view was breathtaking. I went inside, called room service, and asked for two beers to be delivered to my room. Minutes later, my mom's slider opened, and she peeked out.

"I thought I heard your door open. Mind if I join you?"

"I'd welcome the company." I grinned. "What a view, right?"

"It's magnificent, honey."

A knock sounded on my door just as Mom sat down.

"I'll be right back." I answered the door and thanked the steward, whose nametag read "Carlos," for the beer. I felt bad that I had no money to offer him as a tip. Mateo had cleaned both of us out. After grabbing two plastic cups, I carried them and the beer to the balcony and took my seat next to Mom. "Here we go." I cracked open her beer and poured it then did the same with my own. "Cheers, Mom. We made it out alive."

She tapped cups with me, said she loved me, then turned her attention to the water, looked out, and smiled. "This is heaven on earth, Mitch."

I followed her eyes and watched as the final rays of the orange sun dipped beneath the Caribbean. "It sure is, Mom. Remember the last night on the ship? We sat on the balcony and enjoyed our beer together."

She sighed. "A lot has happened since then. I prayed for our lives, and God answered my prayers. Now we're able to watch the sun set and the stars come out again. I'm so thankful."

We sat in silence, drank our beer, and appreciated what we had.

Ten minutes later, a knock sounded at the door. I assumed Rue and Royce were back, but it was room service. The same man rolled in a cart loaded with nearly everything on their supper menu. He held up his hand as I was about to apologize again for the lack of a tip.

"It's been taken care of, sir. No worries. Enjoy your meal."

Rue and Royce walked in just as Carlos left.

"Great timing," Rue said. "We've got new clothes for both of you, and I bought some antibiotic ointment for all those cuts you've got on your face and knuckles. You don't want to get any jungle infections, buddy."

"Thanks, guys. I sure appreciate everything you've done."

Royce nodded. "No thanks necessary. We'd all do the same for each other. Enjoy your meal, and we'll talk in the morning. Have a good night."

My boss and best friend walked out. Tomorrow, everything would be explained, but at that moment, we needed nourishment, and then we would make those emotional phone calls home.

Chapter 55

A gentle breeze blew across my skin, and I thought I was dreaming. I opened my eyes and saw that I was in a hotel room with the window open, then it all came back to me. We were safe, Mateo had been captured, and we would go home tomorrow. Today would be spent getting Mateo processed out of Mexico and back to the US, where he would immediately be jailed at the Habersham precinct. I couldn't think of anything that would make me happier other than being reunited with my family and Gus.

My body ached, but I kept that to myself. My aches and pains were small potatoes compared to what could have happened. I knew our kidnapping was my fault, but I couldn't beat myself up about it forever. Mistakes happened because we were human, and that was what humans did— we screwed up at times. I forgave myself and vowed to be more cautious.

I checked the time—nine o'clock. I smiled and couldn't remember the last time I'd lain in bed that long. It felt good. After starting the small pot of coffee, I knocked on Mom's door, and she said she was up. I told her the coffee and I would be on the balcony in a few minutes.

She came out, snuggled up in her plush white robe but looking refreshed. She carried her own pot of coffee too. "I figured we'd need more than one tiny carafe of coffee."

"Good thinking." I stared at the small fishing boats that bobbed up and down with each wave that came in. Some people were already splashing in the water, and others lounged under umbrellas in the sand. "Hungry?"

"Absolutely."

"Yeah, me too. I'll grab the breakfast menu. We can pick something out while we enjoy our coffee. I imagine after breakfast, we'll have to go over everything with Royce."

"That's okay. I don't mind. There's no way in hell I'm going to go shopping alone while you men talk anyway. I'll sit in on everything."

I chuckled. "I'd never let you leave your room alone. Not even to go to the ice machine. We're a damn good team, Mom, and it's going to stay that way."

"Thanks, honey. I like how that sounds."

"How about scrambled eggs, pancakes, bacon, and fresh fruit?"

She nodded her approval. "Make sure they know we need two orders of everything."

"You got it." I went inside, made the call, then returned to the balcony. It was our time to just be, and I relished it. Nothing rushed, no time constraints, just mother and son talking about whatever we wanted to without interruptions. She was right. It was heaven on earth.

At eleven o'clock, I called Rue's room. "Hey, buddy.

Whenever you're ready, we can go over the last few days."

"Okay. Your mom sitting in on it too?"

"Yep. She can handle it."

"Roger that. I'll bang on Royce's door and find out when we need to meet up with the Federales and Dave. There'll be paperwork to go over, and our flight out tomorrow is at two o'clock. I've already contacted the cruise line, and all your belongings are at the port in Tampa, but how do you want to handle your car?"

"Damn, I hadn't even thought of that, but an idea is coming to me that I'll go over with you and Royce when you get here."

"Sounds good."

Rue called me back a half hour later and said they were coming over. Mom sat on the sofa and wore her freshly laundered clothes. Her yellow blouse had a few tears in it, but she said that was fine. Those tears were a good reminder of how fragile life was and how things could turn on a dime. I had to agree.

After they knocked, I welcomed my colleagues in. Mom had already made two carafes of coffee, enough for the time being. Rue and Royce sat at the table, and I sat next to Mom on the couch.

"Just so you know how we figured everything out," Royce said, "we had Tom Branch pull up the text messages between you and Mateo. We saw the accidental message you sent him that was meant for me."

I began to apologize, but Mom cut me off. "It wasn't Mitch's fault. It was mine. I was angry that he was taking time from my birthday cruise to work. He felt rushed and didn't want me to know that he was texting Mateo. Blame me, if anyone."

Royce held up his hand. "Mary, as Mitch's supervisor, I'm to blame. He had legitimate vacation time coming, and I talked him into tracking Mateo during your cruise. It's my fault."

I laughed. "Let's just say nobody is to blame. Shit happens, but in the end, it turned out exactly how it was supposed to."

"With me losing my purse, phone, and wallet?" Mom asked teasingly.

Rue leapt from his chair. "I'll be right back."

My eyes widened. "What the hell?"

Royce smiled. "Rue has something for you, Mary, and I think it'll make your day."

Devon returned with Mom's purse and handed it to her. "We found it in the jungle, where Mateo took you and Mitch. Marie gave me your phone number, I tried it when we were out there, and what do you know? I heard ringing in the brush. There it was, your purse with everything inside."

"Except my money, but that's a small loss. The pictures of my grandkids and all the pictures on my phone are priceless. That's what I care about. Thank you so much, Devon."

"My pleasure, ma'am."

Royce slapped his hands together. "Shall we begin? And no blame anywhere unless it's aimed at Mateo Garcia."

I chuckled. "Amen to that."

We spent the next two hours going over our horrifying experience with Mateo and our time chained up alone. I explained how we'd freed ourselves, only to sleep in an animal burrow the following night.

"That next morning, they found us. I'm not even sure what today is."

"It's Wednesday, Mitch," Rue said.

I nodded. "Well, I'm really glad you guys came looking for us. We'd probably be at the bottom of that cenote otherwise."

"And I'm not a good swimmer," Mom added.

"So, you had something you wanted to share when we talked about your car?" Rue asked.

"Yep, but it's up to Mom to decide."

Mom raised her brows. "I'm supposed to decide what?"

"Well, my car is in Tampa, but we're booked on a flight to Savannah."

She frowned. "That is a problem."

I gave Rue a wink. "I'm thinking Devon and Sarge can escort Mateo back to Savannah, and we'll fly into Tampa. You and I can pick up our belongings and then drive back home in my Corvette. What do you say, Mom?"

"I say hell yeah."

"Good, then it's planned. I'll call the hotel in Tampa and tell them I'll pick up the car tomorrow afternoon. We'll drive home and should be there by dark. I'll let Marie and Meg know to expect us then."

"That's a wonderful idea, honey, and I'm looking forward to spending more time with you."

"Okay. I hate to get back to business, but we need to head to the Federales office and get that extradition paperwork out of the way. A dozen signatures here and there, a summary of your ordeal and the people involved in your kidnapping, and then we should be good to go. I'll make sure the airline is aware that we're transporting a criminal back to Savannah. We'll board first and exit last—typical protocol. I'll get your seats secured for the flight to Tampa, and by noon tomorrow, Mexico will be in the rearview mirror. Also, the cruise lines said they'd have your luggage taken to the Bayview Boutique Hotel, where you can pick it up with your car when you get into Tampa."

"Thanks." I glanced out the sliders at the aqua Caribbean. "Although we have a killer view—excuse the pun—I am looking forward to going home. It's been a long six days."

"Then shall we go?"

I pocketed the room keys. Mom grabbed her purse, and the four of us headed out. After the unpleasant necessities were out of the way, I would take Mom to the marketplace so she could replace the gifts she'd bought for everyone, then we would have supper at an authentic Mexican restaurant. I was looking forward to that evening.

Chapter 56

By five o'clock, we were back at the hotel. The statements had been given, the paperwork signed, and all the necessary calls made. Tomorrow, Pedro would drive us in their van to the airport, where we would go through security, check in through the police entrance, and say our goodbyes. Mateo would sit in a holding area away from all of us until time to leave. After we said a "see you soon" to Royce and Rue, they would escort the shackled killer onto their plane, and we would board our flight for Tampa.

Mom and I spent our last night in Mexico at a beachfront restaurant overlooking the Caribbean. She had two full bags of gifts at her side. Rue was thoughtful enough to loan me his stipend credit card—with Royce's approval—since we needed food and gas to get back to Savannah.

"Look at that, Mitch." Mom pointed beyond the harbor. "See the cruise ship? Look at how beautifully it's lit up. We never had the opportunity to see that on our own ship."

"No, we sure didn't. We didn't get to see the ruins either. Sorry your birthday cruise went so wrong."

She waved away my comment. "It was wonderful if you

take Mateo and his men out of the mix. Think of the stories we'll have to tell everyone."

I laughed.

"Who else do you know who's been in a real jungle like that? And who, besides us, has slept in an animal's burrow? Do you know anyone other than you who has fallen thirty feet into a real cenote? Most people probably don't know what a cenote is."

I noticed how her eyes twinkled when she reminisced. I was certain there wasn't another seventy-year-old woman who had been through what Mom endured and came out unafraid and stronger for it. I was proud of her.

"You looking forward to getting home?"

"Not really."

"No? Why?"

"Because the adventure will end, and I'll be back in my apartment alone."

My heart broke. "Mom?"

"Yep."

"How about a nonstop adventure?"

Her eyes lit up. "What do you have in mind, honey?"

"Move back home. You'll be with Marie every day, and you can help her with her art projects, plus you'll be around the kids and Gus all the time. You know the house is big enough for all of us. We'd have to change the sleeping arrangements, though. The girls are using your old bedroom, you know."

"What's a bedroom? It's where you sleep. Nothing else. I can use a smaller bedroom. Not a problem. Do you really want me back home, Mitch?"

"I can't think of anything that would make me happier."

She reached across the table and squeezed my hand. "Me neither."

Chapter 57

It had been a long day, but we finally landed in Tampa without incident, went to the hotel's concierge counter, and picked up our suitcases. Then I explained that my Corvette had stayed in their lot a few days longer than planned. I was ready to settle up and leave.

"Not a problem, Mr. Cannon, but it looks like you're free to go. Your tab was taken care of by a Devon Rue. Give me one second to get your car keys."

I smiled. "Okay, thanks."

"You've got wonderful friends, Mitch," Mom said.

"I know, and I see a lot of amber ale being stocked at the house. It's Devon's favorite."

The concierge manager returned with my keys. "Here you go, sir. Have a nice drive home."

We had six more hours together in a small car, and I couldn't think of better company. Mom and I talked all the way to Jacksonville, pulled in at the same restaurant as before for supper, then continued home.

I turned in to my driveway at seven o'clock, tired but happy. Meg's car was parked in front of the garage, and all the house lights were on.

"Think they'll be excited to see us?" I chuckled.

"I don't have to think." Mom pointed. "Here they come."

Seven people and Gus ran from the patio door, down the steps, and to my car. They screamed with happiness since we were safe and back home. Everyone chattered. They asked questions and wanted to know every detail and if we were okay.

"How about we go inside to do our talking? We could use a big pot of coffee too."

Meg squeezed me. "It's already brewing, bro."

After bringing in the suitcases and gifts, we gathered in the living room. Mom passed out the souvenirs from Playa del Carmen, although we hadn't really spent much time there. We explained our adventure in the jungle using the best PG descriptions we could because of the kids. Some other time, we would share the real experience with the adults. They were just happy to have us home.

"So, Mom," Marie said, "do you want to go on another cruise?"

"Nope. I'm over that. From now on, we'll rent an RV and go on family vacations together—every one of us, and that includes Gus."

"Really? I didn't think he was your favorite family member," Meg said.

Mom swatted the air. "Come here, Gussy. I'll get used to him. After all, I'm moving home."

I laughed, my sister's eyes bulged, the kids cheered, and Gus wagged his stub of a tail.

"I'll be back in a half hour, guys. I have someplace I need to go."

Mom gave me a wink, and I left for the precinct. I borrowed Mom's phone and used it to call Royce since mine was somewhere in the Mexican jungle.

"Got him processed yet?" I asked.

"Oh yeah. He's just sitting in the holding area."

"Good, I'll be there in five."

Minutes later, I walked into our precinct. I couldn't have been happier to see all those friendly faces again, and I teared up. I quickly wiped the tears away with my sleeve. Pats on the back, hugs, and handshakes came from all of my coworkers. Royce and Rue walked in grinning.

"You ready?"

"I've never been more ready in my life."

"Then let's go throw that piece of shit into his own cell where he belongs," Royce said.

"My pleasure."

We walked downstairs, and Jack and Ben, the guards, had Mateo shackled and on his feet. Hatred filled his face when his eyes met mine. He cursed all of us, then I nodded to Jack.

"Put this killer in the worst cell we have. Make sure it doesn't have any windows either."

"That would be number seven."

"Go ahead." I followed Jack as Mateo was pushed forward into his cell. He turned as if he was going to headbutt me, but I was prepared. My fists were cocked and ready to go. "You sure you want to try something, asshole?"

He grumbled and took a seat on the cot.

"This is one of the best days of my life. How does it feel, Mateo? If nothing else, I live up to my words." With that, I grinned, slammed the cell door, and walked out.

THE END

Thank you!

Thanks for reading *Pray for Your Life*, Book Three in the Detective Mitch Cannon Savannah Heat Thriller Series. I hope you enjoyed it!

Find all my books leading up to this series at http://cmsutter.com

Stay abreast of my new releases by signing up for my VIP email list at: http://cmsutter.com/newsletter/

You'll be one of the first to get a glimpse of the cover reveals and release dates, and you'll have a chance at exciting raffles offered with each new release.

Posting a review will help other readers find my books. I appreciate every review, whether positive or negative, and if you have a second to spare, a review is truly appreciated.

Find me on Facebook at https://www.facebook.com/cmsutterauthor/

Printed in Great Britain
by Amazon